ICE

KNIGHTS OF SILENCE MC
BOOK I

AMY CECIL

ICE- Knights of Silence MC Book I

Copyright © 2016

Book cover design and layout by,
Ellie Bockert Augsburger of Creative Digital Studios.
www.CreativeDigitalStudios.com

Cover design features:

Sexy young couple body at night closeup: © sakkmesterke / Dollar Photo Club
Midsection of sexy man pulling denim: © WavebreakMediaMicro / Dollar Photo
Club Wings Logo: © kutukupret / Dollar Photo Club black harley motorcycle: © aon168 / Dollar Photo Club

Editing Services provided by
Carl Augsburger of Creative Digital Studios.
www.CreativeDigitalStudios.com.

ISBN-13: 978-1535251662
ISBN-10: 1535251662

DEDICATION

    This book is dedicated to my husband, Kevin. No matter what, you never doubted me or my abilities. All that I am - you let me be. What a wonderful life for as long as you been by my side.

– I love you baby!

PROLOGUE

1995 – Edinboro, Pennsylvania
Caden

"Higher! Higher! Push me higher, Caden!" Emma giggled, as she demanded me to continue to push her on the swing.

Emma is my friend – actually, she's probably my best friend. We have lived next door to each other for as long as I can remember. I was drawn to her as soon as she was born, even though I was only six at the time. She was so darn cute!

My parents have money, so you could say that I am privileged. However, the only kids that are my own age are from the private school that I attend. Their parents belong to the same country club to which my parents belong. They are all stuffed shirts, and I find that I have nothing in common with them. Emma is different. There is a bond there that I can't explain.

Emma's parents and my parents are good friends, so as she grew, it was only natural for Emma and me to become good friends as well. It is really hard for me to explain my relationship with Emma. At first, I guess I felt sorry for her. Both her parents work all the time and Emma is often alone or with the nanny. So, I decided to spend time with her. Once I started playing with her in the nursery and spending time with her, I found that I really enjoyed being around her. I would teach her things like her ABCs, and we would sing songs together. I know, it sounds silly, but in my younger years making her happy made me happy. Now that Emma is older, I find her to be strong-willed (and, I might add, spoiled rotten). And somehow, that is ok. Our friendship is beyond the point to question it all now.

As I got older, I started feeling like her protector. Someday, she will need me and I'm going to make damn sure I'm there for her, no matter what.

We have played together just about every day for the last few years. She always makes me laugh, and I find that even after all these years, I still always want to be around her. Emma knows now, even as a precocious ten-year old, that I would do anything that she asked of me. She has got me wrapped around her little pinky, and she knows how to use that fact to her advantage. So, when she asks me to push her higher on the swing, naturally, I do it.

I turned sixteen last week. My father says that I am becoming a man now, that I need to spend more time with grownups, and that I need to start thinking about my future. He thinks I spend entirely too much time with Emma. He believes that my relationship with Emma is unnatural because of our age difference. He says my feelings for her will change. When I asked him how, he just says that one day I'll feel different about her than I do now. It frustrates me, because I don't understand.

Dad and I will never see eye-to-eye on things. We are nothing alike, and honestly, sometimes I think that there is no way he could be my dad. My mom, on the other hand, totally gets me. She and I have more in common. We both love the outdoors, while my dad prefers to be inside, either working or reading. Mom is more social, like me, and we both know the importance of good friends and spending time with family. We also have a bit of rebelliousness in us and don't see anything wrong with doing things that aren't always accepted or considered normal by our society.

I remember one time a few years ago, Mom, Dad, Ari and I were having dinner together at the country club. On this particular evening, the after dinner entertainment was Karaoke. Mom and I wanted to stay but Dad was ready to leave. Mom pleaded with Dad to let us stay and reluctantly, he agreed. We listened as several people got up and sang. Some were better than others. Some had no business singing in public. Mom, Ari and I laughed and sang along. Dad was just annoyed by it all. It was clear to me that Mom wanted to sing. "Mom, you should go up and sing" I encouraged her. Dad immediately responded, "What are you talking about Caden, your mother can't sing. She will embarrass herself, not to mention all of us." Well, that remark only made Mom more determined. She got up from her seat and looked directly at me and said, "Come on Caden, let's sing." I immediately followed her. We sang "Don't Go Breaking My Heart," by Elton John and Kiki Dee. We were a huge hit, everyone applauded us, but Dad was not happy. He insisted that we leave as soon as we were done. Dad was so mad at us. I don't think he spoke to either of us for a week.

And then there was the time I got caught after hours skinny dipping in the country club pool with Amber Carrington-Higgins. Amber was the club president's daughter and of all the girls I could choose from to skinny dip with, she was probably the worst choice. Her dad made a point to make an example of us both and never missed an opportunity to publicly humiliate us. Dad was livid, said that I was an embarrassment to the family. Mom tried to reason with him, saying that I was a typical teenage boy. She even went as far as to remind him of what he was like at that age. It didn't work. Dad just couldn't see it the way she saw it.

I find I can talk to Mom more easily about things, too. I've talked to her about Dad's feelings regarding my relationship with Emma, and she said that my dad thinks that there will come a time when Emma's friendship will not be enough for me and that I'll want a romantic relationship with her. To an extent, I can see her point. I've often thought about Emma being older and us actually dating. But I also know that Emma is just a little girl and those thoughts are preposterous. She is just too young.

My five-year-old sister, Ari, loves Emma. She looks up to her like a big sister and Emma totally loves Ari. However, Ari always wants to hang with us and sometimes, even though Emma enjoys having Ari around, I find that she gets a little jealous at times when it is not just the two of us. Personally, I like it better when it is just Emma and I too. Ari can be annoying at times and I find that I don't have the patience with her that I should. She is that annoying little sister who wants to do everything with me and I don't want to be bothered. Now don't get me wrong, I love my sister, but I really do not need to hang out with her. She is much more like my dad. Dad spends more time with her than he ever does with my mom or me. Dad and Ari will sit together in his study for hours. Dad will be working, while Ari has one of her books pretending to work along with him. It is really cute to watch the two of them; they are two peas in a pod, as my mom always says. But for me, she is just too much like my dad for me to hang out with.

"Caden, why did you stop pushing me? I'm not flying anymore!" Emma squealed.

Realizing that I'd been lost in thought and not giving Emma her required 100% of my attention, I started pushing the swing again. After several minutes of this, my arms began getting tired. "Emma, do you mind if we head back home? Haven't you had enough of the swing today?"

"No!" She cried, "Just a few more pushes? Pretty please, Cade?" I love it when she calls me Cade. I'm such a sucker!

"Fine, but just a few more and then we are going back. I have stuff to do today. I won't be able to spend all afternoon with you."

After a few more pushes on the swing, I let the swing start to slow and descend. When the swing stopped Emma jumped off and grabbed my hand. She looked up to me with her big blue eyes and said, "Why can't you spend the day with me? I thought today was our day?"

I smiled and said proudly, "I spend just about every day with you. But today, I can't. I'm sixteen now and I have grown-up stuff to do." It was cool being sixteen. Dad was right about one thing; I was becoming a man, and the first thing on my list was to get my driver's license.

"What kind of grown-up stuff?" she asked with her nose upturned.

"Well, if you must know, I'm going to take my driver's test today. After that, I have to go into town and meet with my dad at his office."

She laughed. "Oooh, Caden is gonna be driving," she teased. Then she tried to wink at me and added, "Now you can start taking girls out on dates." After she said this, I noticed that her smile suddenly faded and she started to frown. Her nose crinkled up and her eyes looked as if she was about to cry.

"Now Emma, take that frown from your face. You know you are my only girl," I reassured her. I knew that was what was bothering her. Emma has this strange fascination that I will marry her when she gets older. When I try to explain to her that I'm too old for her, she just gets upset and pouts. It's easier to just play along. I figure she will understand better when she's older. I mean really, what harm could it do to play along with her fantasy?

She giggles and asks, "Does that mean that you will take me on dates?"

"Of course," I replied. "We can keep coming to the park, but we can drive instead of walk like we do now. Or, if you are really good, we can even drive to get ice cream."

"Ice cream!" she squealed. She then added, "I think I would like an ice cream date." That was all she needed to hear. Her smile returned and we started to walk back to her house. A few minutes passed and then Emma asked cautiously, "Caden, why are you meeting your dad in town?"

Damn. I'd known this question was coming. I was dreading it, and had been hoping that we could just avoid this conversation altogether. But Emma, being Emma, didn't miss anything – and deep down, I'd known she would catch on. I just didn't want to break the news to her that I will most likely be working for my dad's firm, and that would mean that we can't spend as much time together. We usually spent every day together during our summer vacations, but this year, Dad wanted me to work. He made that perfectly clear last night during his "you're a man now" talk.

"Well son, tomorrow is your big day. You are a man now. What are your plans for your future?" he'd asked.

Stunned by his question, I responded, "Dad, I'm only sixteen. I haven't really given my future much thought."

My response obviously angered him. I could see his brow furrow and his temples pulsate. He always got this way when he was angry, which was usually when he was talking with me. If you haven't figured it out yet, my dad and I don't get along at all.

"That is what I expected. Caden, you have no ambition and no drive. I am so disappointed in you. How do you expect to be a man without any plans for your future? How do you expect to support a family?"

"Dad, I'm sorry. I just haven't thought much about any of that. I have plenty of time to make those decisions. I'm sorry I disappointed you," I responded the only way I knew how so as to not anger him more. Dad was not abusive to me physically, but his words always made me feel unworthy of the Jackson name. He always made me feel as if I didn't belong.

He was quiet for a couple of seconds and then he said, "Caden, don't be sorry, do something about it." He paused for a moment and then added, "Never mind, I have already taken care of things. Tomorrow, after you take your driving test, you are coming down to my office. You will start working for me."

Surprised by his plans for me, I argued, "Dad, I don't want to work for you. I have no interest in investment banking."

"Well, what are you interested in?" he asked.

"I don't know; I have never really given it much thought. But I know that I don't want to be an investment banker. Please Dad, just give me some time to think about it."

"No, you have had sixteen years to think about it. You will go into investment banking and follow in my footsteps. I will make a man out of you yet. You will have finally done something that makes me proud of you. I don't want to hear another word about this. I've made my decision."

The finality of his words felt like a pit in my stomach that weighed down upon me, not to mention the fact that the comment about finally being proud of me made me feel like crap. My mom saw my hurt feelings and frustration and tried to intervene, but he put his foot down and we both just remained silent, bending to his will as always.

Lost in thoughts of last night's discussion, I was brought back by Emma calling my name.

"Caden? Caden, you didn't answer me," she stated.

Hesitantly, I tried to explain. "Well, peanut, I've been meaning to talk to you about that." Her frown returned. Shit. I'd known this was not going to go well at all, and her frown indicated that the decline in her mood had already started. But I had to tell her, so I continued, trying to break it to her as gently as I could. "You see, Dad wants me to work for him this summer. So, I'll be getting a job." My dad has a very well-established practice in town. It's the last thing I want to do, but if Dad has it his way, it will be my legacy. Nothing would make him prouder than for me to follow in his footsteps. So, basically, I'm doomed to be a paper-pusher for the rest of my life, just to make my dad happy. Lucky me.

"A job? Will you have to work like Mom and Dad do?" she asked sheepishly. "They work every day, except Saturday and Sunday. I never see them, I'm always with Marissa, my o pear," she said, struggling over the foreign words.

I had to laugh. "Emma, she's an Au Pair, not an O Pear."

"Oh," she said a little embarrassed. "I thought I was saying it right." She's quiet for a moment, and then she added, "So, am I right? Are you going to be too busy for me?"

Sadly, I replied, "I'm sorry, sweetheart, but it looks that way." I don't like this anymore than she does. Dad and I argue about it constantly. He keeps telling me that I should not be spending my free time with a little girl, and that I need to start working toward my future. He further explains that working at his firm would be the perfect opportunity for me to spend time with *grown-ups*. Shit, *grown-ups*! He was going to have me spending time with a bunch of snobby bankers and I was going to hate every minute of it.

Emma's eyes started to well up with tears. She stopped walking and asked, "When will I see you?" The look on her face broke my heart. She took several deep breaths and then, turning away, she yelled, "I'm never going to see you!"

I reached for her arm and turned her back to me. She looked down at the ground, refusing to look up at me. I touched her chin and lifted her head to make her look at me. "Sweetie, I promise. I will make time to see you. It just won't be as often." I hope she knows I have every intention of keeping that promise. I added, "Look at it this way: because we won't see each other so often, it will make our time together more special."

Her expression shifted from despair to anger in a matter of a second and she exclaimed, "I don't like it!"

"Emma, please try to understand. You know this is what my dad wants. I don't like it any more than you do. Do you really think this is what I want?" She shook her head. "Of course not, but please understand. I don't have a choice. You know I have to do what my dad says."

She then asked the question I kept asking myself: "If this isn't what you really want then why can't you tell him that?"

I smiled. I know some day she will understand, but trying to explain this to a child...well, I know it will get me nowhere. So, I responded with the only thing I could think of: "It's complicated."

"It seems pretty easy to me; you just say 'Dad, I don't want to work for you.' Yep, looks pretty easy to me."

I had to chuckle at the simple way she looks at things. I've always envied Emma's relationship with her parents. I know they will support her in whatever she chooses to do with her life. But unfortunately for me, it never has been and never will be that simple for me. When it comes to something my dad wants it's always been his way or no way. "Emma, you know it is not that easy for me."

Emma pouted. "I know you have always said that, but I still don't understand. You are only sixteen. Your parents have lots of money, why do you need to work?"

Defeated, I replied, "Oh Emma, I don't know. It's just how it is supposed to be. At least, that's what Dad keeps telling me."

Just then, Emma and I hear a loud rumble coming from behind us. We instantly recognize the noise, and Emma cowered behind me. Coming down the road were about five Harleys carrying members of the Knights of Silence Motorcycle Club, referred to by most as the MC. The MC rules our small town of Edinboro. Or perhaps "rule" is the wrong word...they've established a presence in town, and unlike what most others felt, I always felt safer when they were around. They never messed with the residents in town – in fact, it appeared to me that they maintained order in our quaint little town. Most folks felt differently, believing that the MC was a menace and brought nothing but crime and chaos. I've never seen that. From what my mom told me, things were much worse before the MC came.

Before the Knights came to Edinboro, the Satans MC pretty much ruled our town. They took over just about every business, forcing the business owners to pay them for protection. They harassed civilians that were not involved with the MC. The crime rate was at an all-time high, and Edinboro suffered a murder rate of that of a big city. Then one day the Knights pushed the Satans out. I really don't know how, but one day the Satans were gone and the Knights took over. This all happened before I was born, and my mom has shared this with me. She seemed to have a fondness for the MC that I never really understood, but commented on several occasions that she had gone to school with some of the boys in the MC. They were her friends. To her, those friendships meant something – however, my dad felt completely differently. He thought the members of the MC were a bunch of criminals and hellions.

The MC never bothered me, but for some reason they terrified Emma. She leaned in to my side and held her hands over her ears until they passed by. I, on the other hand, was the exact opposite. The MC fascinated me. From what I understood, they made their own rules. By contrast, I still lived by my dad's rules. It's not that my dad was a bad parent – he just had my life planned out for me. It didn't matter what I wanted.

I watched the bikes pass in awe. Having that kind of freedom – not to mention a Harley – would be a dream for me. But I knew better. Owning a motorcycle was not in the cards for me. The freedom of the open road was something that I could only wish for. I was bound to enter the corporate world. My dad made sure of that.

Once they passed, Emma stepped away from me and said, "I don't like them. They are scary and their motorcycles make loud noises. It hurts my ears. Mama says that they are bad men."

She was probably right about that, but I really didn't know for sure. Edinboro is a small college town with a resort type of community. The town is a borough of Erie, located in the Snowbelt of Lake Erie. I swear, I don't think there are more than 7000 people in the town. The MC kept us straight and kept the crime from the bigger city away.

They all wore matching leather vests with lots of patches. They wore so many patches, it was hard to figure out what they all mean. One in particular always intrigued me: a black patch with a white diamond on it. Inside the diamond was a single 1%. One day I was curious as to what that meant, so I Googled it on the web. 1% basically meant they were not always law-abiding citizens. I decided it was best not to share that information with Emma, but I also didn't want to agree with her comment. The MC kept to themselves, and there was never any crime directly linked to them, only speculation. I truly believed that they would never hurt an innocent person. Mom told me that they just maintained order, and I believed that. "Emma, I don't know if they are bad or not, but we should not judge them," I replied with the only response that seemed fair.

Emma and I continued to walk home. When we got to her house, she gave me the biggest hug. "I'm going to miss you so much! I love you, Caden Jackson! Please don't forget about me."

Hugging her back, I replied, "Oh sweetheart, I could never forget you."

Emma

After Cade dropped me off at home, all I wanted to do was go to my room and cry. I could not believe that he was going to start working. I'd never see him. He said that he would never forget me, but I just knew he would. He was growing up, and he was going to leave me all alone.

I watched him walk back over to his house and just stood there for a short time wondering what things were going to be like without my Cade. The tears welled up in my eyes again and I decided to just go in the house. When I got inside I found Marissa, my *Au Pair,* sitting at the kitchen table.

"What's wrong, sweetheart?" she asked.

Sniffling, I replied, "Nothing, absolutely nothing." Now I was getting angry. This was just not fair. Why did my Cade have to leave me?

"Emma dear, don't tell me nothing is wrong. If nothing was wrong, you wouldn't be crying." She paused for a moment, walked over to me, and hugged me. "Now, why don't we sit down and you can tell me what is wrong."

She pulled out a chair for me and as I sat down I started crying even harder. I yelled, "Caden doesn't want to be my friend anymore!"

Marissa hesitated and then said, "I find that very hard to believe. Caden has been your friend since you were a baby. Why would he not want to be your friend anymore?"

Hiccupping now, trying to get myself to calm down, I said, "Because he wants to work with his dad and not spend time with me."

"Emma, I think you misunderstand. I truly believe that Caden will always be your friend. The two of you have been inseparable since you were a wee thing. But sometimes, people have to do things that they don't particularly want to do. I believe that's what is happening here. I think now that Caden is sixteen and will be driving soon, his parents want him to start thinking about his future."

"No! I'm his future, Marissa! I am!"

"Emma, you need to be reasonable. You are just a little girl. Before you know it, Caden will be graduating from high school, he will go off to college, and eventually get married and have babies of his own."

What was she saying? Didn't she know? Caden was going to marry me! He promised. When I get big, that's what he said. "Marissa, you are wrong! Caden isn't going anywhere, and he is going to marry me!"

"Honey, Caden can't marry you. You are too little. You are just a child."

"No, he is not going to marry me now. He is going to marry me when I get big! He promised!"

"Come here sweetie, I think you and I need to have a girl-to-girl talk."

"What's a girl-to-girl talk?" I asked.

"Well, it's when two girls have a grown-up conversation." I got up from my chair and went to her. Marissa wiped the tears from my eyes and then started our girl-to-girl talk. "I want to explain something to you, and hopefully you can understand this. Caden is a sixteen-year-old boy. He has so many things to do with his life, like I mentioned before." I started to interrupt her and tell her that was not going to happen, but she put her finger over my lips and stopped me. "Please let me finish. You need to understand and accept this. What you feel for Caden is an infatuation. All little girls go through this with an older boy at one time or another. When I was little, I had a cousin that was older than me and I told everyone that I was going to marry him one day. When I got older, I realized how foolish that was. That's what you are feeling now. Caden has been your hero, your prince, for as long as you can remember. It's only natural that you look up to him and idolize him in this way. But as you get older, you will see that Caden was and always will be your friend and nothing more. You are old enough now to understand what I am saying. Do you?"

I didn't like what she was telling me. I *was* going to marry Caden, but I thought it best to just agree with her. I nodded in agreement and turned to the doorway. I looked back at her and said, "Thank you, Marissa," and then turned and headed to my room.

Well, that helped. At least I learned one thing from that conversation: I don't like girl-to-girl talks.

Present Day - 2015

Caden

Twenty years ago, I told Emma that I could never forget her. I didn't realize how true my words were that day. For twenty years I haven't been able to get her out of my mind, no matter how hard I've tried. I haven't spoken to her or seen her for about eleven years, but that doesn't mean I haven't missed her. After all that has happened between us, she is and will always be my Emma, at least in my mind. There isn't a day that goes by that I haven't wondered how she is or what she is up to. Today is her birthday, and she is in the forefront of my mind more than ever. She would be thirty now. I think back to that wonderful summer day we spent at the park. She was so young and innocent...that's one of the last happy memories I have of her. In those days we were innocent and everything was easy. But as I started working and Emma grew up, things got complicated. It seemed that there was always tension between the two of us. Suddenly, we were arguing all the time. Then, everything just went to shit. I have nobody to blame but myself, but that still doesn't make it any easier to bear.

When my feelings for Emma first began to change, I didn't understand why every time we were together I would become angry with her. Eventually I realized that I was falling in love with her. Suddenly, I wanted to be with her in different ways. I knew it was wrong on so many levels, and my weakness made me so angry. She was just a teenager, and I was a man. As my feelings continued to grow for her, an odd tension arose between us, and it kept getting worse every time we were together. So, I did the only thing I could think of to ease the animosity between us: I started to distance myself from her. Looking back, this was probably my first mistake. She was old enough to understand, and if we'd just talked about it, all the bad things that followed would not have happened.

In 2001, my parents were killed in car accident on highway 99. You know those freak accidents where the driver of the other car comes out of nowhere, causes chaos, and then disappears into the night? Well, that's exactly what happened to Mom and Dad. It was New Year's Eve, and my parents, Ari, and I were supposed to go to the country club to attend their annual New Year's party. It had been a family tradition for as long I could remember. Unfortunately, Ari had not been feeling well all day and about an hour before we planned to leave, she started running a fever. Mom felt it best that she should stay home, and Mom would stay home with her. I could see the disappointment on my mom's face, as Mom looked forward to this party all year long. They didn't get to go out together much, as Dad was always working. This was always a special night for her. Wanting her to have her special night out with Dad, I volunteered to stay home with Ari.

After Mom and Dad left, I went upstairs to check on Ari. She was sound asleep. I changed back into jeans and a t-shirt and went back downstairs to kick back and enjoy a quiet evening at home. Around 9:30, there was a knock at the door. To my surprise, it was Emma. She said that the party was boring without me and felt she would have more fun hanging with me at home. I was already starting to distance myself from Emma, but really was not ready to completely cut her out of my life at that point. How could I? I loved her. So, we made some snacks and settled down on the couch watching TV.

Around 1:15am, the local sheriff came to our door and told me that my parents were dead. When Emma reached for me to embrace me, I immediately pushed her away and asked her to leave. It was not one of my better moments. I had just received a shock, but it was not right to take that out on her. Reluctantly, she stepped away from me with tears in her eyes, grabbed her coat and purse, and left. She didn't say another word to me. She left me alone. I was alone with dead parents and a kid sister who didn't know that the life she had always known had changed drastically. So there I was, trying to figure out how to break the news to Ari, wanting my best friend there. I was alone. And thanks to my being an ass, I had nobody to blame but myself.

After that night, my friendship with Emma pretty much became non-existent. For some reason my parents' death seemed to make things worse between us. My guess is that pushing her away was the last straw for her. She still tried, but I found it to be the perfect opportunity to increase the distance between us. As much as I needed her, I couldn't bring myself to confide in her. I had nobody. She tried on numerous occasions to comfort me and I just continued to push her away. It became more and more difficult to control the feelings I had for her. I needed her in more ways now, and when she was around, I always wanted more...but she was so much younger than me. I know she was eighteen at the time, but she didn't want me in that way, so I surrounded myself with women who did. Getting laid was never a problem for me. There were always women who were more than willing to satisfy my needs.

The distance that continued to grow between Emma and I didn't seem to deter her, and she was always trying to "reconcile our differences". Whatever the hell she meant by that, I had no idea. She still couldn't understand why I kept pushing her away. When it became clear that Emma was not getting the hint, I finally found a way to break all ties with her. As much as I hated hurting her, it was the only way. One of the last things I remember her saying to me was that she had *hated* me. I know I was right in keeping my distance, but on that particular day, my complete disregard for her feelings drove the final wedge between us. I was just so angry with her for not wanting me the way I wanted her. Thinking back, I wish I had handled things differently. Not only that, I should have. It was my biggest mistake and my only regret.

After my parents' death, life for me changed drastically. I spent many hours trying to sort out Mom and Dad's estate with their attorneys. Eventually, I was told that we had lost everything. Talk about another shock! Dad had made some bad investments and all our money was gone. Everything! Try explaining that to my twelve-year-old little sister. All that was left was Ari and I. Here I was, 24 and in the prime of my life, and I was guardian to a twelve-year-old kid. My life sucked! What the fuck was I gonna do with a twelve-year-old prepubescent kid? We'd lost our family home and were only left with enough cash to get a small apartment in town.

With the money gone, I had to drop out of college. Dad's business had been sold to pay off some of his debts. I suppose I could have gone back to work there, but under the circumstances, I was sure they wouldn't want me. Word had gotten out about Dad's bad investments, and the Jackson reputation had gone to hell. I needed a job. What little money we had left wasn't going to last forever.

I started the job hunt. Talk about no fun. We lived in a small town that consisted of only a few local businesses, such as Betty's

Dinor and the Game Over Tattoo Parlor. Nothing really interested me except the Silent Fix, the Knights' bike repair and restoration shop, but I was sure they weren't hiring. But one day as I passed by the shop, to my surprise I noticed they had a "Now Hiring" sign in the window. I thought, *What the hell?* I couldn't believe my luck. I had no experience, but I was willing to learn, so I went in and applied. After all, what did I have to lose?

As I feared, the first question I was asked was about my experience. Disappointed because I already knew how the interview was going to turn out, I sadly shook my head and said, "No, sir." Then I quickly added, "But I am willing to learn whatever you need. Please, I just need a job."

The guy at the counter looked at me curiously and said nothing for what seemed like an eternity. Finally, he spoke, "What's your story, kid?"

Surprised by his question, I said, "Sir, I am not sure what you mean."

Shaking his head, he replied, "Your story. Plain and simple. Why are you so desperate for work? You're sitting there dressed in your designer jeans; you don't look like you are in need of a job."

I looked down at what I was wearing: my Rock Revival jeans and a polo shirt. I looked like a snob. I understood where he was coming from, but I was still a little taken aback by his assumption of me. "Well, sure, I guess you would think that. But it just proves that you should not judge a book by its cover."

He smirked and said, "So, you're a smartass?"

Pissing him off was not what I was hoping for. I should have just thanked him for his time and left, but a part of me hoped that perhaps I could salvage this. So, looking him in the eye, I responded, "Sir, I meant no disrespect. It's just that I really do need to find a job. My parents passed away about a month ago and I am the sole guardian to my kid sister. We were left with nothing, and like I said, I really need to work."

Recognition crossed his face along with an expression of surprise. "Fucking A, you are Tyler and Katie Jackson's kid, aren't you? I heard about the accident, it was all over the papers. I'm so sorry."

Smiling, I replied, "Yes sir, I am. Did you know them?"

He laughed. "Did I know them? Hell yeah, I knew them. We went to high school together. We hung around together for a time, then things changed." He fell quiet for a moment, appearing to be thinking back to his younger days. He then added nostalgically, "Your mama was a real sweetheart."

I smiled. "Yes, she was. Thank you." There was an awkward silence between us; he seemed lost in thought. I had to know about the job, but I was afraid to break the one thing that was going in my favor today. Finally, unable to wait any longer, I had to ask, "So, about the job?"

Surprised, he replied, "It's yours. I know you don't have the experience we are looking for, but we can teach you what you need to know. You come from good stock, son, it will be my pleasure to show you the ropes personally. But first of all, cut the *"Sir"* crap. Name's Ace." He held out his hand and I shook it. I had a job, and from what I gathered, a mentor. What had started out as a shit day turned out to be the best day of my life.

They hired me to work in their office, checking in customers and keeping up with the jobs that came in. As he'd promised, Ace took me under his wing right from the start. He was the club's VP, and he always said I had potential. He taught me all about the bikes: how they ran, and how to repair them. I soon got to know the other members of the club who worked in the garage. After a year, I was working in the garage on repairs with the other guys and definitely knew my way around a motorcycle, thanks to Ace.

I made it a point to make myself indispensable to the shop and the club. I worked hard and learned everything I could in the shop. If a repair needed done by a deadline, I made sure it was done early. If that meant working long hours, I did it. I loved my job and wanted to keep it at all costs. I even helped the club outside the bike shop.

One night, I was walking home from work when I heard a woman scream. I turned toward her voice and saw a punk kid trying to take the lady's purse. I immediately stepped in; thankfully he was not armed and he ran off. I walked her home to ensure her safety. We got to talking and as it turned out, she was a club member's old lady. She was so grateful and over the next few days, she made sure that the entire club knew what I had done for her. After that, the old ladies in the club really stepped in and took Ari and me under their care. They helped me out with Ari so that she was not left alone when I was working late. They made sure that Ari and I always had meals and looked after us. I soon realized that I was rapidly becoming more than just an employee, I was a member of their family.

One afternoon, the club President approached me. I didn't see him around the garage much, so his presence surprised me, especially when he came directly to me. "Hey Cade, got something I wanna discuss with you."

I immediately stopped working on the bike in front of me and replied, "Hey Red, whatcha got?"

"Me and the brothers have been talking ... well, we are real impressed with you, son. You wanna prospect for the club? Ace says he would sponsor you."

A year ago I would not have had any idea what he was talking about, but hanging around the guys for over a year now, I knew he was asking me to become a potential member of the club. I was honored and wanted to say, *"Hell yes!"*, but I had Ari to consider. Not only that, I had to think about Emma's feelings in all of this as well. We had not spoken much over the last year and a half, but I knew how she felt about the club and my working for them. I was sure that joining the club would probably sever what was left of our relationship. I just couldn't answer him without taking all of this into consideration. So, I replied, "Wow, Red, I am honored. Really, I am. But, I can't give you an answer right now. Can I think about it and let you know?"

He knew my situation, and he understood that I had an underage dependent to take into account. To my knowledge, he didn't know about Emma. "Yes, of course. I know you have that little angel of a sister to consider. How about we do this: you come to the clubhouse Saturday night. We're having a club picnic. The brothers and their families are welcome. We start around four, but around seven, the party is for adults only and the kids are sent home." He winked and nudged me, then continued, "If you know what I mean. I'll make sure we have someone to take Ari home and stay with her so that you can stay and enjoy the party."

I knew exactly what he meant. I had never been invited to a club party, but I had always heard a lot of stories from the guys about the club's parties; they always talked about the drinking and the women. I didn't hesitate. "Thanks Red, I'll be there."

Red nodded, "Good, and I hope you really give the idea of prospecting for us some serious thought. It isn't easy finding good, loyal people to be members of the club. You will be an asset to this club." He patted me on the back and started to walk away, but then turned and added, "See you Saturday."

The party was like nothing that I had ever experienced before. Red was right, it started out as the perfect family affair, but when the kids were sent home all hell broke loose. They guys hadn't exaggerated their stories; the party provided more alcohol and women than I ever imagined. In that one night, I felt more connected to that club than I did with anything else in my life, except Emma. The next day I accepted Red's offer to prospect.

A year later, I was a full-patched member of the Knights of Silence MC, with my very own Harley. Don't get me wrong, it wasn't easy. I worked hard to earn that patch. But once I was patched, life suddenly became a hell of a lot easier! Our club was a good club, for the most part. Yes, we were 1%ers, but I learned over those two years that we did more good than bad. We sponsored several charity rides to help Jerry's Kids and the Make a Wish Foundation, and on several occasions, we held rides against child abuse and even supported several dog rescues. We owned a multitude of legitimate businesses in Edinboro and all across the country. We had several bars, strip clubs, various shops, and trucking companies. While all these businesses provided a steady income for the MC, they also came in handy for laundering money and hiding illegal shipments of guns and sometimes even drugs. The illegal part wasn't our business of choice, but sometimes, we needed to bring additional money into the club and did what we had to do to make it happen. We made our own rules and lived by them. We rode free and partied hard!

Over the next eleven years, our club saw many changes. Prospects came and went; some ended up getting patched while others just didn't make the cut. We had rules, and if a prospect couldn't abide by the rules, then he was out. To hold an office, you had to be a full-patched member for at least two years. All officers were voted in by the club's members. To even be considered for an office, one of the elder members had to nominate you. We didn't mess around when deciding who are leaders were going to be. My first nomination came from Ace, after three years of being patched. After the vote, I then served as the club's Sergeant-at-Arms (SAA).

I was responsible for ensuring that the bylaws and standing rules of the club were not violated. It was my job to ensure that the orders of the President were carried out in a timely and efficient manner, as well as policing and keeping order during all club events. I had the authority to enlist any club member or prospect to aid me in controlling any situation and using any means that I deemed necessary in said situation. Basically, I was responsible for the safety and security of the club, as well as the protection and defense of its members and prospects. I was referred to by most as the club's enforcer, and it was also my job to protect the president, even if it meant giving up my own life.

It was a job I took very seriously, and I held that office for four years – until the Satans returned to Edinboro. Their arrival caused an all-out war between the clubs, and in the aftermath of all that, they gunned down Red, wounding me in the process. When I saw the gun aimed at Red, my instincts took over and I ran to take the bullet. Unfortunately my timing was off and the bullet grazed my shoulder, but hit Red square in the chest. I may haven't been able to save him that day, but I made sure the fucker who killed him didn't live to talk about it.

As Vice President, Ace took over the club and nominated me to sit in the VP seat. We all mourned the loss of Red, but we also wanted revenge. Side-by-side with Ace, the club and I planned our payback. It was a war between the clubs that lasted four more years. We lost several more club members during that time, with the biggest loss to me being Ace. He was the closest thing I had to a father. After Ace died, the club unanimously nominated and voted me in as President.

Three years later, I am still the club's reigning President. The road I have traveled in the last eleven years has not been a cakewalk. I have suffered pain and loss of the worst kind. I paid my dues with blood, but the club that I have grown to love so much has rewarded me tenfold. I have a family, and I'll protect them until my dying day. Ari has twenty-five brothers who reside in Edinboro that would lay down their lives for her. And if needed, there are 150 members from the many Chapters across the country and Ireland that she could call on if she needed them.

Never in a million years did I imagine this would one day be my life. However, if I could go back, I would only change one thing ... the way I treated Emma.

CHAPTER 1

Caden - One month later

Rebel rapped on my office door. "Hey Prez, I think you need to come out front. We've, uh ... got a situation," he said as he stood in the doorway to my office. I looked up to see my Sergeant standing there looking a little out of sorts. Rebel was rock solid. Nothing ever rattled him. What in the hell was going on now?

"What's the problem?" I asked curiously and a little anxious as to what could be causing him to be so unnerved.

"It's a woman, boss," he said hesitantly. Really? You've got to be kidding me. He is letting a sweetbutt get to him? He continued, "She's not a sweetbutt, Ice. I've never seen this chick before." How the fuck does he do that? I swear he knows what I'm thinking before I realize I am thinking it. "She's hysterical," he added. "Says she needs to speak to *Caden*." He said my name as if he knew something I didn't. What the hell?

Nobody calls me Caden, except Ari. Hell, half the members don't even know me as anything else but Ice. Ari wouldn't have been detained at the gate, so that only leaves one other person. Could it be? After all these years, could Emma really be here? At that moment, I stopped thinking. If it was indeed Emma, then something was up and she needed me. I got up from my desk and rushed out of the office and headed toward the front gate. Our compound was gated and always guarded by a prospect or two. We had to maintain security at all times. Many of our dealings were not on the up-and-up, and we knew we couldn't be too careful – besides, we were still having some issues with our rival club, the Satans.

As I approached the gates I almost stopped in my tracks. It was her, my Emma, all grown up and still the most beautiful woman I had ever seen. Don't get me wrong; I have had women, some more beautiful than others. The sweetbutts were always hanging around, and were more than willing to give us guys what we wanted, hoping that we would make them our old ladies. But none of them compared to Emma. I motioned for the prospect to open the gate.

When the gate opened, Emma ran into my arms, crying hysterically. "Oh Caden, it's you! It's really you! I was hoping that I would find you here."

As I held her in my arms, I said with surprise, "Emma, what's wrong? Did something happen?" I held her away and looked her over: checking for cuts, bruises, blood, anything that would give me some indication as to why she was so upset. "Are you hurt?" Still looking her over, I realized that she was ok physically and I pulled her back into my arms.

Muffled into my chest, she said through her tears, "I need your help! You are the only one who can help me!"

I felt that I had died and gone to heaven. Holding Emma in my arms after all this time was like coming home. And she needed *me*! I couldn't even begin to fathom what was wrong; she had led such a charmed life. Rich parents, college … anything she could possibly ask for. But as I held her, she wouldn't stop crying.

"It's ok sweetheart, there there." I wiped the tears from her cheeks and looked into her beautiful blue eyes. "Why don't you come inside and tell me what you need," I said hesitantly. I knew how she felt about the Knights and everything that we stood for. She must really be in trouble for her to resort to my club and me. She stepped back and caught her breath, wiping her tears away with the back of her hand and nodded. I reached for her hand and said, "Come," as I led her inside the clubhouse.

Once we were inside, I took her to my office and motioned for her to take a seat on the couch. Grabbing a box of tissue from the bathroom, I handed it to her and sat down next to her. "Now, why don't you tell me what has you so upset."

She wiped more of her tears away and blew her nose. Then, she began to speak.

"My best friend Brianne is missing." That hurt. I thought I was her best friend. Well, I have nobody to blame for that except myself. "Nobody can find her and she has been missing for days. She left with her boyfriend last weekend to visit her parents. She never arrived home, and her parents called me asking if I had seen her. When I said no, they became really worried. They called the police. The police are saying they are doing everything to find her, but they say that they have no leads. I'm really worried, Cade, and I didn't know where else to go."

"Emma, I am not sure I can help you. Why would you think that I would be able to find a missing person? Why wouldn't you enlist a private investigator for something like this?" I asked, confused. Why would she think I would be able to help her? Yes, we had shady dealings, but I was not in the business of finding missing girls.

And then, Emma dropped the bomb. "I thought about a PI, but then, considering her boyfriend's connections, I didn't think it was the smartest direction to go." Now, I was more confused than before. What did she mean about his connections? She continued with her explanation, "You see, Brianne was dating a member of the Satans Rebels MC. I don't trust the police, because I believe that they are either avoiding the MC or they are in their pocket. Probably the latter, if you ask my opinion, but what do I know?"

Now, I understood. The Satans Rebels MC was our biggest rival. We were constantly feuding over territory, guns, and especially women. Specifically, the way they treated women. They'd come back to our area hoping to get their territory back and expand their club. We had prime territory, only a short distance from Lake Erie. It gave us an advantage in receiving all kinds of shipments. Our club was bigger, but they had big dreams of taking us down and have tried several times to no avail. It was never going to happen – not on my watch. It is my job as president to protect this MC. All our members and Chapters depended on me to keep us all whole. We have hundreds of legitimate businesses that employ members of the MC as well as civilians. I will not let the Satans take over any of our territories. Well, now it was starting to make sense as to why Emma came to me. But now that I know the connection, Emma needs to give me more.

"Ok, so she was dating this guy. What makes you think she is in any kind of danger?"

"Oh, Caden!" she started to cry again.

I needed to get Emma to calm down. She was still very upset and I had to get her to focus and give me all the details. "Emma, I can't help you unless I know everything. Why do you think this guy is the reason that your friend is missing? If you want my help, you need to be honest and tell me everything you know."

She nodded in agreement and took a deep breath getting her tears in check. "About a month or so ago, Brianne started dating a guy that she said was the vice president of the Satans Rebels Motorcycle Club. That threw up all kinds of red flags for me."

I interrupted, "Really, why would the idea of your friend dating a biker be a cause of concern for you?" I looked at her knowingly, and she knew I was baiting her.

"Caden, really, do we need to go there now?" She was right, this was not the time or place to have this conversation. I just couldn't help myself. It had always hurt me that she could never accept the life I had chosen for myself.

"Fine, continue with your story." I was not happy about the fact that she had called me out as being childish without even saying the words. Damn woman!

"A few weeks ago, she brought him to our house for dinner. She introduced him as Skid. What a stupid name. I assumed it was a nickname, but she never introduced him or spoke of him by any other name except for Skid."

"If she only knew," I thought to myself.

Emma continued, "She said that she thought she had found *the one,* and she wanted me and Mark to meet him."

Mark? Who the fuck is Mark?

"From the minute I saw him, I didn't like him or trust him. I knew he was bad news right from the start. He was dressed in leather from head to toe and was covered in those nasty tattoos."

There she goes again.

At her last comment, I looked down at myself. I wasn't in leather from head to toe, but I did have my leather cut on and had several tattoos of my own, though she couldn't see all of them. For now, I preferred it that way.

She immediately realized what I was thinking and quickly said, "Oh Caden, I didn't mean … I'm sorry, really. I didn't mean to offend you."

I had to laugh at her prejudices against all MCs in general. Boy, her mother really did a number on her, feeding her all that bullshit about us when she was younger. Well, at least I know that she still feels the same about my choice of career. She's made it perfectly clear that she still hates the Knights. But you can make damn sure that when all is said and done, her mind will change. I'll make sure of that. Actually, I find it humorous. Now that she needs us, bikers aren't so bad. *But who the fuck is Mark?* This conversation was only making me angry. Her uppity attitude toward us made my blood boil, and I so wanted to set her straight. I was not good enough for her to call her friend anymore, but now that she needed me, she didn't want to offend me. Really? But instead of laying into my anger at her, I decided to let it go … for now. I needed to get to the bottom of this first. I would deal with her later on a more personal level.

Still, I had to ask, "Emma, wait. Before you go any further, let's get clear on a few things first. Is it fair to assume that you still hate bikers?" She opened her mouth to speak, but I was not done, and stopped her by saying, "I'm not finished. Whether or not you hate us, it's easy to see that you don't trust us. It has been years since we have spoken and now that you need help, you decide to come and find me like nothing bad happened between us. Help me out here darl'n, 'cause the last thing I remember hearing from you was that you hated me. I assume that is still true – or has that pretty little head of yours had a change of heart? And who the fuck is Mark?"

The look on her face was priceless. Did she really think that I would jump the minute she came running? Did she think that I wouldn't notice her mention another man's name? Yeah, I know I hurt her bad, but that was for her own good and it happened a long fucking time ago. I would think that now that she is older and more mature, she would understand why I did and said the things that I did.

Finally, once she got over the shock of me calling her out, she spoke, "So, I see you are still a bastard." She got up and grabbed her purse. "I'll find help elsewhere. Thanks for nothing." She turned toward the door and proceeded to leave.

I rose from the seat and called after her, "Oh no! You don't get off that easy." The deep baritone of my voice stopped her in her tracks. She turned to face me with pure defiance on her face. Now, there was the Emma I have known and loved all these years. The feisty bitch was back and I couldn't be happier. "It doesn't work that way, sweetheart. You came here for my help. You knew that I wouldn't say no. You just need to understand that by getting my help, you get the help of all my brothers. If you can't respect them or this club, this arrangement won't work. And yes, I am still a bastard. Get used to it." I paused and added, "I will only ask you one more time: who the fuck is Mark?"

She fidgeted and looked down at her hands. "Mark Grayson." She spoke so softly I could barely hear her. I gave her the look. Realizing I wanted more, she added defiantly, "He is my fiancé – and please stop swearing at me."

Her fiancé? No, no, no, this can't be. I immediately looked down at her left hand and saw the huge diamond ring she was wearing. She caught what I was doing and quickly covered her left hand with her right. I hadn't noticed the ring until now. Why hadn't I noticed it? I was so arrogant to think that she would wait for me all these years … I never believed she would be engaged. Well, she finally did it. She has left me speechless, but I know that I have to say something. Does she even know how she has wounded me right now? I know I should not have expected anything different from her, but I'd always hoped that we would find our way back to each other.

"Ok, Cade, get it together. You still hold all the cards here. It is you she came to for help, not Mark. Use that to your advantage." I asked with as much sarcasm as I could muster, "Your fiancé? I didn't know you had gotten engaged, when is the happy day?"

Looking down at the floor, she replied, "We have not set a date yet."

Trying hard to hide the smile from my face, I added sarcastically, "Well you better be sure to send me an invite. I wouldn't want to miss the party." I added, "Why isn't Mark helping you?"

Quietly, she responded, "He refuses to help."

"What do you mean he refuses to help? That makes no sense."

Shyly, she responded, "Well, when I told him about Brianne, he said that he was sure she was fine. When I pressed him on the issue as to why he was so sure, he basically told me that I needed to mind my own business. He said that Brianne was a grown woman and it was not my responsibility to take care of her or worry about her. He told me to let the police do their job."

"And so you then came to me?" I asked, still trying to figure out exactly why she would go against her fiancé.

"Like I said before, you were my last hope. We weren't getting anywhere with the police and after my conversation with Mark, I decided it was best that I dropped the subject and not discuss it further with him."

Ok, now I am mad. This guy is supposed to love her. "This is the man you want to spend your life with, a spineless bastard that cannot even help his future wife? I just don't get it, Emma. What happened to you over the last 11 years?"

She finally looked at me, really looked at me, and pleaded with tears in her eyes, "Cade, please, let's not do this now. I don't have any intention of discussing Mark with you anymore. I've come to you for help. Can that be enough for now?"

I watched her change almost immediately when I started asking about Mark. Something is up there, but obviously she does not want to talk about it. Or at least, she doesn't want to talk about it with me. As I was about to give her an answer, she quietly asked, "So will you please help me?"

Of course I'm gonna help her. My Emma needs me, what else can I do? I resign myself to drop the subject of Mark, for now. I will get to the bottom of that one down the road. I answer her, "Yes, I'll help you; however, only if you can accept my terms. You want me? Well, the club is a part of me. You can't have one without the other. If you can respect my club and trust that we know what we are doing, then we will help find your friend." Before she could interject, I continued, "That means that you will refrain from expressing your uppity attitude or opinions to me, any of my brothers, or any of their old ladies. You will be truthful in everything you tell us and you will do as you are told. Even if you don't agree! Are we clear?"

She nodded in agreement, then asked, "May I ask one question?"

"Of course," I replied.

"What is an old lady?"

I laughed. I couldn't help it. That innocent little girl came through in her question and I could see that beautiful precocious ten-year-old I remembered. She was so fucking adorable. It was not going to be easy being around her all the time, especially now that she is engaged. The old saying is true: be careful what you wish for. I realize now that it was easier to love her from afar. I'm so fucked!

"Emma, you are definitely going to need some MC training. Especially since you will be staying at the clubhouse for a while."

"What? What do you mean, staying at the clubhouse? I can't stay here. Mark will never allow it."

"Remember the part of our agreement where we talked about you doing what you are told?" She nodded, her eyes downcast. I continued, "Yes, you are staying here. Don't ask me why, but my gut is telling me there is more than meets the eye with the disappearance of your friend. I just can't put my finger on it right now. I would feel better if you were here, where I can keep my eye on you. If Mark Grayson loved you, he would agree and *allow it* as you say. Hopefully it won't be for long and you can return to your charmed life." I paused briefly, then added, "Oh, and don't call me Caden. I haven't used that name in years. It's Ice now; you will do well to remember that. Now, I am going to get my VP and Sergeant and bring them in here. I want you to tell us everything about your friend." As I started toward the door, I turned back and said, "Stay put, I'll be right back." I couldn't help noticing the amused expression on her face. What's up with that shit?

CHAPTER 2

Emma

"*Ice?*" Is he serious? I couldn't help but laugh to myself. Ice what? Iceberg, Ice chest, Iceman? Oh, this is just too funny. Iceman would fit him. I know he has been to hell and back, but that doesn't give him the right to act like an asshole.

He was right about one thing, though. I did tell him I hated him. Even when I said it, I didn't really; I never could. Caden had always been there for me for as long as I can remember. By the time I turned sixteen, I was crushing on him big time, but he kept pushing me away. He no longer had the time to spend with me, nor the inclination to make the time. It broke my heart. He is still so hot, with that dark hair, ice-blue eyes, and that sexy smile. *That's it! That is where the nickname came from! I get it now.* Seeing him after all these years, I forgot how much I had been missing him. The day I told him I hated him was the worst day of my life.

I had seen Caden around women, lots of women, especially after he joined the MC. But I had never actually seen him *with* a girl. We had not seen each other in a long time and I was missing him so much. He no longer lived next door and his absence was always in the forefront of my mind. He knew I was mad at him for joining the Knights, so we pretty much kept our distance. Right before I left for college, I decided that I was finally going down to the MC to talk to my friend – if he still wanted to be my friend, anyhow. When I got to the gate, I asked if I could speak with

Caden. A couple of the guys at the gate talked in hushed tones to each other. I couldn't make out most of what they were saying, but I did hear one say, "But she is just a kid." Despite his objections, they decided to let me in. They told me Cade was in the clubhouse. I went inside and was immediately appalled. The clubhouse was filthy and smelled of beer and cigarette smoke. It was disgusting.

Still, I was determined to find him. I asked one of the girls at the bar where I could find him and she directed me to his room: upstairs, last door on the left. A little nervous, I walked up the stairs and headed for his room. The door was ajar, so I stepped in. There he was, sitting in a leather chair in his room while some whore sucked him off. He was combing his fingers through her hair and moaning. I gasped and couldn't move. He must have heard me because he looked directly at me and smiled. There I was, staring at my dearest friend in the whole world, and he was staring at me while that bitch was finishing him off. I was so hurt. Tears started to stream down my cheeks. I could not look at him anymore and took off. I ran as fast as I could, but when I got to the gate I had to wait for the guys to unlock it and let me out. As I waited, I heard him calling after me.

I refused to turn around. I couldn't face him. The guys started to open the gate, but when they heard Caden yelling they stopped. I felt a strong arm grip my shoulder to stop me. I couldn't take it. I tried to think of a time when it was just us, when he loved me, but the vision of him and that whore would not escape me. When I finally looked up at him, his gaze was fixed on me and I could see embarrassment on his face.

"Emma, what the fuck are you doing here?" he yelled.

He was angry with me!? He acted as if I was the one who had done something wrong. Oh no, I was not going to allow that to happen. I yelled back, "What do you think I am doing here, asshole? I came to see you. It has been months since you have been around and I was missing my friend. Obviously you weren't missing me, so fuck off Caden. I'm done!"

I turned to leave again, and again he grabbed my arm. "Whoa there, sweetheart. Don't you yell at me. You were the one that barged into my room. You should have called first."

"I have called. You never answer your phone. I even sent you a text to let you know I was on my way."

He looked guilty. "What's the matter, Caden, did I hit a nerve? Don't you have anything to say to me?"

He was still silent.

I was so angry and so hurt! "Who's the whore, Caden? Is she your new flavor of the day? I'd say flavor of the month, but these days you have a new skank every day. It's disgusting."

I knew my words pissed him off, but I was too mad at him to care. I could see the anger radiating from his eyes as he pulled me into him. I'll never forget the feel of him against me. It was more than I could bear, and I remember that my entire body tingled. I was sure he was going to kiss me, and to my surprise I wanted him to.

Our lips were so close, nearly touching as he said, "Get this straight, Princess: when I fuck, where I fuck, and who I fuck is none of your business." He gestured toward the erection bulging through his jeans and continued, "You want a piece of this, you just say the word, sweetheart, and I will be happy to oblige."

We stood there for what seemed like several minutes, but when I think back, it was probably only seconds before I remembered the bitch I had just seen him with and I suddenly felt cornered. When I started to squirm in his arms, he released me. My anger rose beyond its boiling point and I yelled, "It will be a cold day in hell before I would ever want a piece of *that*! I hate you, Caden Jackson!" I turned toward the gate and left. My heart was shattered, and I swear I cried for three weeks straight.

That was the last time I spoke to Caden. He deserved my anger because he was so cruel to me, but we should have talked since then. As I look back on that day, I have come to realize that I was jealous. Seeing him with that skank made my heart literally ache. He was mine! He was my Caden, my prince ... and the Knights MC took him from me. He had changed. He was no longer the sweet, attentive boy I had grown up with, and I blame the MC for that. He had become someone I no longer recognized. That's why I hated the MC and everything they stood for, not because they were outlaws. I had to laugh at myself. What a predicament I have gotten myself into now. I just didn't think; my first instinct was to go to him. When I was younger and I was in trouble or needed something, I always turned to Caden. Mark won't help me, and he is going to be furious that I have asked Cade for help. But, if I want to find Brianne, I am at the mercy of the Knights of Silence MC and Mark Grayson is just going to have to live with that.

Just then, Caden – I mean, Ice – walked back into the room, followed by two big burly guys who I assumed were his VP and Sergeant. Caden gestured for the men to sit and then introduced them as his VP Hawk and his Sergeant Rebel. I don't think I'll ever understand the MC name thing. Both men nodded a hello to me – or at least, that's what I thought it was. Caden then asked me to tell them my story about Brianne, which I did. I told them about Brianne and Skid, leaving out my opinions of course, as I had promised.

When I finished, Rebel spoke first, "Prez, what the fuck? Why are the Satans taking women now?" I realized that he was addressing Caden – I mean, Ice. He is their president. All this time talking with him, I never noticed the President patch on his vest, which now I see plain as day. Rebel continued, "Really Ice, do we really want to get involved with this?"

"Reb, I have no idea why the Satans are doing this, but I think there is more here than we know."

"I hear ya, I do, but at the same time, I can't help but think about the last time we tangled with the Satans. We lost lives. I'm not sure the boys are ready for that again."

Hawk jumped in, "I agree with Reb, Ice. I'm not convinced that we should get involved." I was beginning to worry. Were these guys going to talk Caden out of helping me? I sat there nervously listening to their conversation and anxiously awaited Caden's decision.

Caden quietly listened to their arguments and seemed to take into consideration what they were saying. Once they voiced their concerns, Caden spoke. "Look guys, I totally get where you are coming from. Do you really think that I want to endanger our boys? Of course not, you both know me better than that. But I also think it is important for us to make sure we keep tabs on the Satans. The last thing we want is to be blindsided by something they have done. They have been quiet for far too long, and it worries me."

"Do you think they know the connection between Emma and Brianne, and Emma's connection to you?" Hawk asked.

"I didn't even consider that this might be personal," Rebel added. That thought never crossed my mind. Could this be personal? I waited for Cade's response. I was curious what he thought about this.

"Good question, but I'm pretty sure they don't know the connection between Emma and me. We were childhood friends, but we've been out of touch for many years now. So I don't believe this is personal, but on the other hand, I believe that it is something that we should at least look into. Don't ask me why, it's just a gut feeling that I have that tells me not to let this one go." He looked over to me and seemed lost in thought until Rebel spoke again.

"Your 'gut feelings' are usually right on, Prez. If this is something that you feel strongly about, I'm with ya."

"Thanks, Reb." Caden looked over to Hawk and asked, "And you? I need you both. If I don't have you both behind me on this, there is a good chance that I'll not get the rest of the club to agree to at least look into this."

Hawk smiled and said, "Hell yeah, I'm with ya. You're my Prez, and if you believe that this is something we need to do, then I'll stand behind you. So, what's the plan?"

"I don't have anything definite yet, but I have been thinking about this for some time, but it never seemed like the right time. This situation with Emma gives me the reason I have been waiting for. I think that we should send someone in undercover and see if we can get any info. Someone outside the club, it can't be a member. Ideas and suggestions would be helpful here. I'm not going to the table without a plan in mind."

Rebel nodded his head in agreement.

Hawk said, "I think it's the best move to make right now, since we don't have a lot of information."

It sounded really dangerous to me, but I trust Cade. And I really had no idea what he meant by "taking it to the table", but I was sure I was about to find out. Caden nodded, and it seemed that all three were in agreement.

Caden stood and said, "Reb, get Tiny and Honey in here. I need their help getting Emma situated. She will be staying at the compound until this mess gets straightened out. Hawk, let the boys know: church in 15." He then turned to me and said, "You stay put; I'll be right back." He saw my defiance and he gave me that look that said, *"You better not say one word and do as you're told."* I immediately refrained from speaking and just sat there. He commanded these men with such confidence and authority. He was beginning to scare me and turn me on at the same time.

My feelings for Caden run deep. As a little girl, he was my knight in shining armor, my prince, and I was sure I was going to marry him when I got older. But as I got older, I realized how girlish those thoughts about Caden were. As I became a woman and grew old enough to know the difference between girlish ideals and physical attraction, my feelings for Cade changed drastically. Plain and simple, I wanted him. When I saw him with other women, it broke my heart. The more I wanted him, the more he pushed me away. Now, seeing him with such control and strength (not to mention that the years had been more than kind to him), I not only wanted him, I needed him.

A few minutes later, Caden walked back into the office with a younger guy and a girl in her late twenties. Before I could say anything to any of them, he said, "Emma, this is Tiny and Honey. Tiny will go back to your place with you to get your things. Just the necessities, please; we don't have room for your whole fucking bathroom." He paused, expecting me to complain, but I didn't. He was testing me. I showed him that I could be compliant by not protesting. He then continued, "Once you get back, Honey will get you set up in one of the rooms upstairs." He then looked at Honey and said, "The room next to mine will do." Honey nodded, although she looked disappointed. I'm sure she was one of his regulars. She looked like a streetwalker, dressed in her skimpy halter-top and short shorts, with her ass cheeks showing. So disgusting. She was, however, very pretty. She had long blonde hair – natural, I would guess – and a tall, slender figure. I was instantly jealous of her.

He then added, "Boys, spread the word: Emma is off-limits!" I could only guess what he meant by *off-limits*, but I had to chuckle to myself; he is still my protector, no matter what has gone down between the two of us. His men nodded in agreement. When he was done, he said, "Tiny, get moving."

Tiny approached me and said, "Miss Emma. If you are ready to go, ma'am?" He was so polite. Tiny was short, about 5'6", but built like a brick house with sandy blond tousled hair. He was very attractive, in a boy-next-door kind of way. I giggled to myself as I realized how he'd got his name; he was anything but *tiny*!

"Yes, I'm ready," I replied as I got up to leave. Before I left the room, I turned to Caden and said, "Ice ... thank you. You didn't have to help me, and I just want you to know that I truly do appreciate it."

He smiled at me, but said nothing. Well, that should at least earn me some brownie points, I hope. I left Caden's office, following Tiny.

CHAPTER 3

Caden

After Emma and Tiny left, I just shook my head trying to figure out why I agreed to this. I looked up to find Honey just standing there staring at me with concern on her face.

"Ice, are you ok?" she asked timidly.

I smiled at her. I know what she was thinking, and she was right. Honey has been taking care of my boys for five years: cooking, cleaning, laundry – whatever my boys and I need. She has also been my "go to" girl for several months now. I wasn't planning on making her my old lady, but it was nice to have one steady girl instead of a different sweetbutt each night. With Emma here, Honey has clearly come to the conclusion that our time together is coming to an end. She sees Emma as a threat. How couldn't she? I have never been able to hide my feelings where Emma was concerned.

"Yeah, I'm ok. This business with Emma just has me on edge, that's all." I knew she wanted to say more, but she just nodded. I continued, "When Emma gets back, I'm counting on you to make her feel welcome. She isn't familiar with our lifestyle and has many misconceptions about us. You need to help her understand. Are we clear?"

"Yes, Ice, I understand," she replied with her eyes downcast. I know she was hurting and wanted to have *the* conversation; I just couldn't do it now. She then added, "Just so I am clear, you want me to set Emma up in the room next to yours?"

Shit, I knew she would latch onto that. My room was at the opposite side of the clubhouse and there was only one other room in that wing of the building. The room in question will now be Emma's room. If I was smart, I would put her in the room farthest away from mine, but I just couldn't. I replied, "Yes, you are correct." I know she wanted me to elaborate, but that just wasn't going to happen. "If you will go now and get things ready, I would appreciate it."

After Honey left, I headed to the chapel. When I got there, my boys were all waiting for me. I took my seat at the head of the table, Hawk at my left, Reb seated at my right. I banged the gavel and church was on.

"Thank you all for getting here so quickly. A situation has come up that I think needs our immediate attention. Some of you may be wondering who the lady was that was here earlier. Her name is Emma Baylee and she is an old friend. I know this goes without saying, but where Emma is concerned – hands off! If I catch any of you harassing her in any way, I'll have your head. Are we clear?"

Reb looked at me, confused. "Ice, you are right, that does go without saying. I don't believe there is a brother at this table that would mess with another brother's woman."

"Absolutely," Hawk added. "We respect our brother's women."

They were right. "I know, but I guess I'm a little overprotective where Emma is concerned. She isn't mine, but I don't want any of you to think that she is up for grabs. You all got me?" I asked again for confirmation. They all nodded in agreement. I continued, "Her friend Brianne has not been seen for several days now. The last Emma saw her, she was with Skid Row of the Satans. Knowing what we know about the Satans and how they treat their women, I think there should be real concern here if they have Brianne." The boys all looked to me in shock. They understood my reasons for wanting to get involved with this, not to mention that this particular situation hits close to home considering my friendship with Emma.

We may be an outlaw club, but I did my best to keep my club as clean as possible. Don't get me wrong, we love the illegal shit – as long as civilians don't get hurt. Plus, we never involved women. We still dealt in guns and occasionally drugs, but we tried to concentrate more on our legitimate businesses to keep the club going. The last thing we wanted to do was to rely on the income of our illegal activities to keep the club lucrative. The Satans, on the other hand, dealt with every illegal fuckery that they could get involved with. They would not think twice if a civilian got caught up in one of their deals and they treat their women like whores and punching bags, all the while prostituting them out for a quick buck. They're known to slap their women around just to prove a point. We didn't harm women. It was one of our absolute rules. If a brother was caught physically or mentally abusing his old lady or one of the sweetbutts, it was grounds for him losing his patch. It was that serious in our world. So, when I mentioned that Emma's friend was with Skid, the brothers knew where this was going.

"Prez, we talking about a rescue mission into the Satans' compound?" Spike asked.

"Well, it may come to that, but for now, we don't know that she is there. My suggestion is that we plant an informant inside the Satans' organization. It would have to be someone who could feed them information about us to gain their trust. They would have to trust our guy completely for this to work. Plus, we could use this situation to our advantage. The informant will not only help us find out what has happened to Emma's friend, but may be able to help us take down the Satans once and for all."

Rebel chimed in and said, "Prez, who are you thinking of? You know it has to be someone who owes us, but also someone that the Satans would not connect to us."

"I agree. Whoever we plant will have to be smart and know how to play the game. I don't have any ideas at the moment – any suggestions?

"What about Skeeter, boss?" Hawk asked.

Skeeter was our superstar. He's a civilian who works in the computer science department at Edinboro University. He was a whiz on the computer and could create programs for just about anything. He got his name 'cause he was exceptionally good at skeet shooting. To look at him, you would never know that he enjoys killing birds, but he loves it. The club helped him out years ago when his dad passed and his mom was having a hard time making ends meet. We found her a job and hooked Skeeter up with the university. Skeeter and his mom have been good friends of the club. They've even come to some club events, but most of our contact with Skeeter happened long before the Satans came back to town; they would have no idea of his connection with the club. He was perfect.

"I like it. What do you all think?"

For about twenty minutes, we talked it over, Hawk, Reb, and I answering their questions when we could. Finally the plan was taken to a vote and passed. I was to make contact with Skeeter and to convince him to be our informant.

I made the call that afternoon, and Skeeter agreed to meet with me the next morning. It was pointless to have the whole club involved in the meeting, so I decided that Rebel, Spike, and Ryder would go: Each one brought an element that ensures you are covered all around. Rebel is my Sergeant and always has my back, Spike loves the kill, and Ryder is the brain of the three. It worked for us.

CHAPTER 4

Emma

Back at my apartment, Tiny helped me get my things in order. I needed to tell Mark something about where I was going, but I just didn't know what to tell him. Anymore, I didn't know how to talk to him without making him upset or angry with me. At one point, I believed that I truly loved Mark. In the beginning he charmed me. He had such a boyish, innocent manner about him that I couldn't resist. But lately, he has been different. It's very hard to explain. He gets angry easily and seems to be on edge all the time. I've even noticed that if I mention Caden in any way, he becomes even angrier, which I do not understand. He doesn't even know Caden. At first, I attributed his behavior to stress from work, but lately, I am not so sure that's the reason behind it. Sometimes I feel that perhaps his true nature may be surfacing. I believe he is jealous of my non-existent friendship with Caden.

So, sure that I wanted to avoid speaking with him about this, I took the coward's way out and just sent him a text, then silenced my phone. I just could not face him; he just wouldn't understand. I was still hurt that he would not help me find Brianne. He didn't know that I had gone to Cade for help and he would be furious to know that the MC was involved. I wrote that I needed space and that I was just going away for a few days – hopefully it would not be longer than that.

Mark knew about Caden. He knew that we grew up together as the best of friends. He assumed that we just drifted apart. I never told him what happened between Cade and me, or of my feelings for him. I had never expected to see Cade again and truly believed that nothing would ever develop between us. But seeing him again, I realize that I still love him and always will. I care for Mark, I really do, but he will never claim my heart the way Cade has. Cade claimed it years ago. It has and will always belong to Cade. I said yes to Mark's proposal because I really thought that we were good together. He is nothing like Cade, and maybe that's what drew me to him. He was different, and I guess you could say I used him to forget about my one true love. But now that I've noticed these significant changes in him, I've been having second thoughts. This angry man that I am engaged to scares me now, and I have become very good at keeping him at arm's length. I guess that's why I have been having trouble committing to a date. Seeing Cade today and having all those memories flood my mind again, I don't think I'll ever be able to marry Mark, even if nothing develops between Caden and me.

When we arrived back at the clubhouse, Tiny showed me around. I never really paid attention to my surroundings when I was here earlier. The smell … yes, the whole place smelled of stale beer. When we entered, I noticed a large room that resembled a bar and game room combined. They had a beautiful oak bar shaped like a "U" with barstools all around it. The room contained three pool tables, video games, and a large flat-screen TV mounted on the wall. In that portion of the great room, there was a myriad of old furniture. Behind the bar was a kitchen, with a large oak table in the center. To the left of the kitchen was a stairway. As Tiny was showing me around, I asked, "Where does that stairway go to? Is my room up there?"

"No ma'am, that's where the boys and sweetbutts sleep. Your room is at the other end of the building, near Ice's room." He smiled sheepishly as if he knew something I didn't.

"Oh, I did not realize I would be separated from everyone else."

"Prez's orders," he replied, with a shortness in his tone that he hadn't had before.

We walked back through the kitchen and back into the great room. On the other end of the great room there were three doors and a staircase. As we passed, I asked, "Where do these doors lead to?"

"You are a curious one," Tiny stated, and then he added, "The first door is our chapel."

"You guys have a chapel here! That's great, when are the services?" I was so excited that this place had something good.

Tiny started laughing; not just a little laugh, but the kind of laugh that makes your eyes water. I did not understand what was so funny. He said, "Miss Emma, you have a lot to learn. The chapel is for church, but not the kind of church you are thinking. That's where we hold our meetings. Members only, and no women."

"Oh, I see," I replied, embarrassed. I realized at this point that perhaps I should just keep my mouth shut. Tiny never elaborated on the other two doors and I didn't ask. I had embarrassed myself enough already. Tiny led me up the stairs to a small hallway with two closed doors. He gestured toward the first door we passed and said, "This is Ice's room."

"Good to know," I thought to myself. I definitely don't want to accidently walk in on him again. Who knows what he would be doing.

When we finally got to the second door, Tiny opened the door and said, "This here is your room."

I stepped inside and was a little surprised at what I saw. The room was clean. There was a queen-size bed on the center wall, with a nightstand on each side, but no lamps. Actually, there were no lamps at all in the room. The only lighting the room afforded was the overhead light with a ceiling fan. On the opposite wall was a dresser, and in the corner I saw another door, which I assumed was a closet. In the other corner was another door, which was open, and I could see it was a bathroom. Relief washed over me: my own bathroom. I'd been so afraid I would have to share a bathroom with the entire MC.

Tiny didn't say anything for a while, letting me take in what would be my new home for the next few days. After I had looked everything over, he said, "I'll go get your things and bring them up. I will be right back. You stay put." He turned and left the room.

I should not have come here. I should have figured out another way to find Brianne, but it was too late now. I have probably plopped myself down right in the middle of a biker war – not to mention the war I was gonna have to face with Mark.

As I was looking around the room, I checked out the closet. It was a decent size for a short stay. It reminded me of something that you would see in a hotel room. The bathroom, on the other hand, was not something you would see in a hotel; at least, definitely not the kind of hotels that I was used to staying in. There was a sink, toilet, and shower. No bathtub, no vanity, it was just very simple and plain. *"It is only going to be a few days,"* I told myself. As I turned back toward the door, I noticed another door on the opposite side of the room. It was closed. I walked over and tried to open it, but it was locked. *"Where does this lead?"* I thought to myself.

Just then, Tiny returned with my bags. "I think I got everything, Miss Emma."

I smiled. He really was so polite and sweet. His personality definitely did not fit the menacing man standing in front of me. "Thank you, Tiny. I really appreciate all your help. And please, just call me Emma. There is no need to be so formal with me."

He shuffled his feet for a second or two, unsure what to do next, and then said, "Well ma'am, if there is nothing else, I should be going."

As he turned to leave, I called out, "Tiny, one more thing." I pointed to the locked door. "That door is locked. Where does it lead?"

Tiny smirked and said, "That leads to the Prez's room." He turned to leave the room, and over his shoulder he added, "Miss Emma, if you need anything, please do not hesitate to ask. I would suggest, however, that you stay here until Ice returns."

I nodded, "Thank you, Tiny. I will." I guessed he would just have to get used to not calling me Miss Emma.

Tiny left. And then, I was alone.

CHAPTER 5

Caden

I decided to run out to pick up a few things that I thought might make Emma feel more comfortable. I knew staying here would be difficult for her, as I was sure that my clubhouse didn't have all the amenities she was used to. When I returned, I had several bags that contained new sheets for the bed, blankets, a new pillow, bath towels, and a couple of lamps. Nobody ever stayed in that room; it was pretty stark. I just wanted to make her feel a little more comfortable. I had no idea how long she would be here. I know she only expected a couple of days, but I guessed it would be longer. And if I was being honest with myself, I was hoping that it would be much longer. I was looking forward to us reconnecting, even if it was just in friendship.

I left the bags in the car and went inside. I noticed some of the guys hanging around watching TV. Rebel and Tiny were at the bar, and Honey was pouring Reb a shot of bourbon. I walked over to greet them and asked Tiny, "Emma all settled in?"

"Yes sir," he replied. "I even carried her bag in for her, so I assume she is upstairs unpacking her things."

"Good, thanks. There are a few bags in the Jeep, please bring them in and put them in my room." I then turned to Honey and said, "Pour one for me? I sure could use one."

Tiny headed out to my Jeep and Honey poured that shot. I looked over to my sergeant, shot in hand, and said, "Drink is the feast of reason and the flow of the soul." We downed our shots and Reb looked at me, shaking his head. I looked at him and said, "What?"

"Where do you come up with that shit? Drink being a feast and flowing into the soul ... what the fuck does that mean?"

"Hey, don't knock Alexander Pope!"

"Who the fuck is Alexander Pope?" Rebel asked, laughing at me.

I just shook my head. These guys just didn't get it. "Never mind. I don't have the time or the patience to explain it to you. I'm going to check on Emma." Rebel was still laughing at me as I left the bar and headed for her room.

As I approached Emma's room, I suddenly became nervous. What if she didn't want to see me? What would we say to each other? It had been so long. Hesitantly, I knocked on her door. I could hear her shuffling about and then the door opened.

"Caden, you're back? Tiny told me that you had to leave. Come in." She opened the door and I stepped into her room.

"I picked up a few things for you. I know this room isn't what you are used to, so I was hoping that what I got would make you feel a little more comfortable."

"You did not have to do that. I won't be here very long – I'm assuming just a day or two. Don't you think?"

Shaking my head, I answered her honestly, "I don't know, but I doubt it. Hopefully we will put our plan into action in the next day or two. But I have learned over the years that these things take time. The more information we have prior to acting, the better the outcome will be. I am not sure I want you out in the civilian world while we are doing this. You are much safer here, and I plan on keeping you here as long as I need to."

"Cade – I mean Ice, sorry – I can't stay here indefinitely. I told Mark I would only be gone for a few days, I have my work, and what about Mom and Dad? They don't know that I am gone. What do I tell them?"

"First of all, you can call me Cade. You don't have to call me by road name. I was wrong in correcting you earlier – actually, I kinda like it when you call me Cade. It reminds me of a happier time. You were the only one that ever called me Cade, and it grew on me over the years. Secondly, I really think that your connection to Brianne could potentially put you in danger. That's why I am keeping you here. You know that I would never do anything to hurt you." She looked at me with a wide-eyed expression, and I knew exactly what she was thinking. I continued, "Ok, besides that." My past mistakes will always come back to haunt me.

She was frustrated with this situation. I could understand that. But how do I make her understand that she is potentially in danger and that I am not willing to take the risk of her getting hurt? Surely she knows I would always protect her.

"Emma, please try to understand. I cannot give you any firm answers on anything right now until I have more intel. Once I get the information I need, then I'll know how to proceed. I will not risk your safety or the life of your friend without having as much information as I can get. It isn't how I operate. My instincts are telling me to proceed with caution. So for now, just know that there is more to this than what we know and I am doing everything in my power to protect you both. Don't ask me how I know these things, it's a gut feeling that I can't explain. But in my experience, my gut feelings are usually right on."

Exasperated, her shoulders slumped, "I understand. It's just that my entire life is being shuffled around, and I have obligations. You can't expect me to change everything."

"I can and I do. If you want our help, you will stay here for as long as I need you to. Understood?" I would never forgive myself if anything bad happened to her. My gut did tell me there was more to this, but I was also acting out of selfish reasons as well. I was just not ready to let her walk out of my life just yet. Especially to marry an asshole who can't even help her. What kind of man does that?

Defeated, she nodded. I left her room and went to get the packages in my room. When I returned she was sitting on the bed staring at the wall. As I entered the room, she turned and saw the bags. She said excitedly, "Oh! What did you buy?"

"Don't get your panties all wet; it's just a few things to make your stay here more bearable. You've got sheets, towels, blankets, and a pillow. Oh, and some lamps. I left them in my room. Let me get them." I left to get the lamps, and when I returned, she was going through the bags I left on the bed, crying. What the fuck? I swear I'll never understand women. "Emma, what's wrong, why are you crying?"

"Nothing is wrong," she replied through her tears. "All this time that we have been apart, I really believed that the club had changed you. But now, I realize that you haven't changed at all, have you?"

Smiling, I replied, "I have changed. I have changed quite a bit. You just haven't seen it yet."

"Well, you are still taking care of me. That has not changed," she said sadly.

"Emma, we may have not spoken to or seen each other in years, but that doesn't mean that I won't be there for you when you need me. I'll always take care of you." Feeling a bit awkward and not sure what to say after that, I began to fidget. After a few seconds, I said, "Well, I guess I better let you get settled. If you need anything, I'm next door. Dinner is at 6, so please feel free to come downstairs and join us. It's not formal, but it is a meal." She nodded and I turned to leave. I had to get out of there before I pulled her into my arms and did something we would both regret.

CHAPTER 6

Emma

I have never felt more alone than I did the moment Cade left my room. There was something so nostalgic about being around him again, even though our conversations were so much more awkward than they were when we were kids. I've missed him so much over the years, even though he was so mean and hateful to me near the end. I wonder what changed. He doesn't seem mean and hateful now. He's actually been very kind to me, agreeing to help me and involving his entire club to do so.

What's the deal with this club, anyway? From what I have seen, these guys are nothing like I expected. They have really surprised me. Yeah, sure, they voiced concerns at first about helping me out. I wouldn't have expected anything less. But their willingness to help a total stranger has really impressed me. And, they have all been very polite to me. They sure don't act like a bunch of outlaw bikers.

Cade and his club are doing more for me in this situation than Mark. So, why am I still engaged to a man that I am not in love with? The more I thought about this, I realized what I always knew, but never would admit. I love Cade. I've always loved Cade. Now what in the hell am I gonna do about it?

Shaking my head, I decided that I wouldn't worry about that now. I'd have to deal with my feelings later. My priority was Brianne.

Not long after the dreadful day I caught Caden with the whore, I left for college. We had not spoken to each other since then. There were so many times I wanted to call him, talk to him, see him … but after our last words, I knew he didn't want to have anything to do with me. I still can't believe that I am here. Coming here was the last thing I wanted to do, but I have been so worried about Brianne, and I knew Cade wouldn't let me down.

In college, Brianne was always there for me. Cade really broke me, and it was Brianne who got me living again. At the time, the only thing I concentrated on was my classes. Brianne would force me out. Most of the time I did not want to go, but after a while, I started to enjoy myself and forget about the hurt that Cade had caused. So now, if my suspicions are right and Brianne is in trouble, I owe her. It's my turn to be there for her and do what I can to help her.

I looked at my watch: 5:15pm. I had decided that I was not going to hide in my room all the time that I was here. If Cade wanted me to accept his brothers, then I needed to spend time with them. Dinner was at 6, which gave me some time to finish getting my things in order, freshen up a bit, and head down to dinner.

Wearing my favorite skinny jeans and a black halter-top, along with my favorite black heels, I headed downstairs for dinner. When I got to the bottom of the stairs and turned toward the kitchen, the main room was filled with members of the MC and several scantily dressed women. Trying not to make any eye contact with any of them, I looked for Cade. He was nowhere to be found. As I headed over to the bar, I saw Tiny sitting there drinking a beer.

As I approached, he said, "Hi there, Miss Emma. Are you all settled in to your room now?"

I smiled again at his politeness. "Yes, Tiny, I am. Thank you for your help today. I really appreciate it."

He nodded. "No thanks necessary, ma'am; just following Ice's orders."

"Speaking of Ice, have you seen him?"

He replied, "Yep, he's in the kitchen at dinner." He gestured toward the kitchen. I thanked him and headed that way.

When I walked into the kitchen, I saw the last thing I'd expected. Several brothers and ladies were seated around the big table. They were passing food, talking, and laughing. It was like a big family dinner. Caden was at the head of the table, an empty chair to his right and Honey to his left. I knew it; she must be his old lady.

I stood in the doorway, not sure of what to do, when Cade looked up and saw me. He smiled, pointed to the chair next to him and said, "Emma, come have some dinner." I walked over to the chair and hesitated. "Darlin', it's ok, please sit. If you wait any longer there won't be any food left."

I nodded and sat down. Cade started passing food to me. There was roast beef, mashed potatoes, broccoli, and salad. Again, I was surprised; I didn't think these guys would eat so well. After filling my plate with more food than I could possibly eat, Cade said, "Eat up. The roast is really good."

I began to eat and after the first bite, I realized that he was right. It was probably the best roast I had ever eaten, tender and juicy. I interrupted the conversation and stated, "This meal is amazing!"

Honey chimed in and said, "Thank you."

She must be the cook. Great. Not only his old lady and beautiful, but a great cook too.

Cade looked over to Honey and smiled, "You've outdone yourself tonight."

Oh my God! She blushed! Then she batted her eyes and said, "Thanks, Ice. I aim to please; you know that." She then nudged his shoulder as if there was some secret between the two of them. Suddenly, I lost my appetite. Maybe I need to rethink my plan to stay here and get to know these people. I can't watch Cade and Honey together all the time. It's just too hard!

After dinner, some of the guys sat around the table talking, while others dispersed to the common area. When I got up to excuse myself, Cade got up as well and said, "I think I'll join you." I smiled at him, and then looked directly at Honey. She looked disappointed. I know I shouldn't have been, but part of me was glad. As Cade and I walked out of the kitchen, he placed his hand in the small of my back as if to lead me out.

"Would you like me to show you around?" he asked.

"Thanks Ice, but Tiny already did." I wanted to spend some time with him and talk, but he seemed preoccupied. Still, I thought I would take a chance anyway and asked, "I'd love a drink, though. Care to join me?"

"Sure," he replied and guided me to the bar. We sat down at the bar and he asked, "What'll you have?"

"Strawberry daiquiri?"

He laughed and then said, "Sweetheart, you aren't gonna find those foo-foo drinks here. Your choices are beer, whiskey, bourbon, or scotch."

Embarrassed, I replied, "Beer would be just fine, thank you."

He then called over to the bartender, "Prospect, two beers." The man named Prospect nodded and pulled two glasses from under the bar, then grabbed two bottles of beer and brought them over to us. "Thanks, Scratch," Caden said, leaving me totally confused. I thought his name was Prospect? Cade could see the look of confusion on my face and then asked, "What? What's wrong?"

Whispering to him so that nobody else could hear, I asked, "I thought his name was Prospect, but then you called him Scratch?"

Cade laughed, something I seemed to make him do quite often. At least I was not making him angry. "Prospect means that he is not a full patched member of the club. He is earning his way to his patch. Sometimes I don't always remember the newbies' names and I refer to them as Prospect. Most of the guys do. But his name is Scratch."

"Oh, I see," I replied. "I assume that Scratch is a nickname, like Ice?"

He smiled at me, his beautiful blue eyes sparkling, and said, "Yes; and it is called a road name, not a nickname."

Again, feeling out of sorts for not understanding his world, I nodded and said, "Ok. I'll try to remember that." I needed a notebook; it would help me get everyone straight while I was here. "Cade, do you have a notepad or a notebook?"

He looked at me quizzically, "What the hell do you need a notebook for?"

I knew if I told him the real reason he would just laugh at me again, so I thought it best to make something up that didn't sound so dumb. But I couldn't think of anything that sounded good, so I stumbled. "Well ... I just like to write things down."

Confused, he shook his head and said, "Yeah, sure."

"Thank you!"

"Remind me before you go up and I'll get you one from my office."

By the time I finished my beer, I was feeling out of place. The boys had started playing pool and watching TV, joking and laughing with one another. Cade stayed with me at the bar, but I got the feeling that I was cramping his style with my presence. So, when I took the last gulp of my beer, I got up to leave. Cade grabbed my arms and asked, "Where you going?"

I turned toward him and said, "I'm a little tired. It's been a long day for me. I think I will turn in."

For a minute, I swear he looked disappointed that I was leaving. But I am sure that it was just my imagination and hopeful thinking playing tricks on me. He then said, "Well, if you are tired. Let me get that notebook for you. Come on." I followed him to his office where he grabbed a notebook and pen from his desk. "If you need anything else, you know where to find me."

"Thanks, Ice. I really appreciate all you are doing for me and Brianne." I then turned to head upstairs to the solitude of my room. At least I had my notebook and I could now make notes on the things I learned. Perhaps his world isn't as bad as I thought. I'm still a bit unsure of all of this, but I am starting to feel that if I learn more about his world, there may be a place for me in his life. I rolled my eyes to myself. What am I thinking? I'm already trying to figure out a way that I can remain here with Cade. Hell, I don't even know if that is something he wants. I'm sure he is hooking up with Honey. He's already taken. He wouldn't want me.

CHAPTER 7

Caden

After Emma had gone upstairs to her room, I finished my beer, got another one, and took it to my office, motioning for Rebel and Hawk to join me. We were meeting with Skeeter in the morning to discuss our plans for him. We needed to be prepared and devise a plan that would get him in quick and out safely.

After a couple of hours of working through the details with Reb and Hawk, we felt we had a good plan that would work.

"Well boys, this has been exhausting. I think I'll call it a day. Don't forget, Reb, we ride at 10. We are meeting Skeeter at Betty's at 10:30am." He nodded and I headed for my room. I have a house on the outskirts of town that I never stay at except when Ari is home from school. I feel it is important for her to have a home to come back to, but I am most comfortable in my room at the clubhouse.

When I got to the top of the stairs, I debated on whether to check in on Emma. It has been a couple of hours ... she is probably asleep by now. I headed for my door, when I heard a shriek and a bang coming from her room. Alarmed, I headed straight for her room and opened the door. There she was, standing in the middle of the room in her short pajama shorts and tank, holding a tennis shoe in her hand. She looked fucking amazing and I wanted nothing more than to lay her out on that bed. But I refrained and asked, "What the hell happened? Are you all right?"

She looked at me shocked; I guess somehow she didn't hear me burst into her room. "Oh my God, Cade, you startled me!"

"I startled you? What the fuck, Emma! Why are you making all that racket?"

She shrugged and said, "It was a spider." I just looked at her in surprise. She had always been terrified of spiders when she was a kid, but I would have thought that she'd outgrown that years ago. I started to laugh. She scowled and added, "Cade, don't laugh at me! You know I hate spiders."

I couldn't help it, I laughed some more. "Did you get it?"

Triumphantly, she said, "I sure did!" She was so damn proud of herself and so fucking adorable. Then she added, "Would you mind disposing of it for me?"

Shaking my head, I said, "I cannot believe you are still afraid of spiders. And that you are still afraid to dispose of a dead one." I walked in the bathroom to get some toilet paper and came back out. "Yes, I will get rid of it for you. I guess some things will never change between you and me."

"No, they won't," she replied, suddenly seeming sad. I threw the spider away and turned to leave.

"Cade?"

"Yeah?"

"I was ... well, I was wondering if we could talk a bit? If you are not too busy, that is."

I wondered what this was all about ... she seemed nervous. "I'm always busy, darlin', but I've got some time. What's up?"

She walked over to the bed and sat. She patted the spot next to her, inviting me to sit as well. As I walked over to the bed, she said, "So, how have you been?"

That was not what I was expecting her to say. "I'm good, actually. Doing better than I have been in a long time." She was the reason for that. I finally had my Emma back in my life. I'm about to face a war with the Satans but because I have reconnected with my Emma, I couldn't be happier. Still, she doesn't need to know all that.

"That's good, but that isn't really what I was asking. It's just ... what has been going on in your life all these years? And how did you end up here – as president, no less? I mean, I know why you joined the MC, but I never believed you would stay in this life."

"Why do you think I joined the MC?" I asked. I know she believed she knew my reasons, but in all actuality, I was sure she had no clue.

Surprised by my question, she responded, "Well, you love motorcycles and you always liked the club." She hesitated for a minute – thinking of more reasons, I'm sure – and then added, "Not to mention, it is the exact opposite of what your dad wanted you to do."

I chuckled at her reasons. She was right about two things: yes, I love motorcycles and yes, this life isn't what my dad wanted for me. But, they were not my reasons for choosing this life.

"Emma, there is something that you don't seem to understand about me and my club. First of all, this club saved my life, as well as Ari's. These men took me in when I had nothing. They gave me a job when I needed it the most. This club has always had my back, and they know I would give my life to save one of my brothers, just as they would do for me. It's as simple as that. There is a loyalty here that you have yet to understand. There are no questions about loyalty. It's a brotherhood and a family, for me as well as for Ari. We had nothing when I became a part of this club, and I'll never forget what this club has done for Ari and me. My club is and will always be my first priority. Maybe after spending time here, you will come to realize this."

"Maybe I will, someday, but right now I just don't understand how you could leave what you knew for this."

"*This*, as you put it, is my life. That will never change." I know that she still does not understand, but hopefully someday she will.

She looked over to me and placed her hand on mine and said sadly, "I've missed you."

Shit! I didn't want to have that conversation with her now. I am not ready to tell her how I feel about her, nor did I want to expand on the fact that I had thought about her every day we've been apart. Did I miss her? You bet your fucking ass I did. But do I tell her that? No, now isn't the time to bare my soul. I need her to accept the club first. I refuse to risk my heart if she can't live this life. Instead of answering, I changed the subject. "What have you been doing the last eleven years?"

She chuckled and replied, "Well, not long after we last saw each other, I went off to college. That is where I met Brianne. She was my roommate, and we worked it out so that we roomed together all through college. Eventually I graduated, and now I work as a consultant for various companies as a reputation manager."

"Reputation manager? What the hell is that?" I had never heard of a reputation manager.

"Well," she said, "it's a PR job. Companies hire me to fine-tune their online presence by strategically tweaking their website, social media platforms, and search results to make sure they have a positive image. It's fun."

"I assume you are paid well for that?"

"Yes, very well. And the best part is that I work from home. Speaking of which, I'll need to get my laptop. I thought I would only be here for a day or two, and didn't think I would need it. But I have a deadline coming up in two weeks and it would probably be best if I got it."

I was proud of her. She had done well for herself. "Sure. We can send Tiny over there to get it." I paused and added, "So, it sounds like you like your job."

"I do," she said excitedly. Then she added, "What do you do?"

"What do you think I do?" Her question surprised me. I would have thought it was obvious what I do.

"I don't know ... I mean, you are president of the club, but you have to make money somehow."

Her naiveté of what we did here didn't surprise me. She had a lot to learn and understand. "You got it right; I run this club – on the Chapter level and on the national level. The club owns several businesses in town, and it is my job to make sure everything runs smoothly. I'm a very busy man, Emma. I have a lot of responsibility, and many brothers, their old ladies, their children, and civilians depend on me."

Embarrassed, she responded, "I didn't realize. What do you mean by Chapter and national levels? Are there more of you?"

"Yes, we have Chapters in twenty-six states, as well as several Chapters in Europe."

"And you are the president of all of them?" she asked, astonished.

"Yes, babe, I am."

"And you like your job?"

"Do I like it? I fucking love it!" Maybe she will get it one of these days. Maybe she will understand this club is my life. Maybe she will even want to share it with me?

She was silent for a moment, then said, "Cade, you never explained to me what an old lady is."

"No, you are right, I didn't. I was hoping that you would have figured it out by now, but I guess I'll need to explain." I paused for a moment while she waited patiently. I continued, "Woman are not allowed to be members of the club. The only way women are permitted into the club is if they are an old lady or a sweetbutt." She opened her mouth to speak, but I already knew that she was going to ask what a sweetbutt was. I held my hand up and continued, "Just hold tight. I'm sure my explanation will answer your questions. Old ladies are like club royalty. They have to be chosen by a member of the club. When the club member makes a woman an old lady, she becomes his property. She can't be shared anymore. Sweetbutts, on the other hand, are shared. They service the boys' needs, when and where any club member wants. They do as they're told, and hope that a brother will make them an old lady. Some old ladies are wives and some are not, but even if they are not married, they are treated as if they are wives. The old lady is loyal to the club member and does not sleep around."

When I finished, she didn't say anything for several minutes. She just sat on the bed and looked down at her hands, fidgeting. Then she looked up to me and asked, "Is Honey your old lady?"

Surprised by her question, I wasn't sure how to respond. Honey was not my old lady, but she had been my regular for some time now. I had been struggling with the decision to make her my old lady for the last couple of months now, but could never convince myself fully that it was the right thing to do. I looked over to Emma and said, "No, she isn't. Why do you ask?"

"She just seems special to you. You call on her for help, she cooks dinner for the club … I just assumed that you were a couple. That's all."

I know I shouldn't have asked this, but it came out anyway: "Would it bother you if she was?" I cannot believe that just came out of my mouth, but I really needed to know.

She didn't say anything at first, and then she said quietly, "It would."

Did she really say what I thought she did? Would it be so obvious if I asked her to repeat it? I needed to know that I heard her right, but I decided to refrain. It was probably best to just leave it to rest between us. "Well, I better head to bed. I have a long day tomorrow and need to get some rest." I got up from the bed and started to head to the door. Hesitating, I turned and walked over to her and kissed her forehead. "Goodnight, princess. Sweet dreams." She looked up at me in utter shock. She didn't say anything; she just stared. Holy fuck, what did I just do? It just came so naturally that I didn't even think about it before I acted.

She didn't say anything at first, and I immediately turned toward the door to leave. Then I heard in almost a whisper, "Goodnight, Caden."

I got back to my room, unable to believe what I had done. Emma didn't seem to be fazed by my action, except for her silence. What's up with that? Then, when she whispered goodnight to me … I wonder if she expected me to hear that? When we were kids, kissing her forehead was a very normal thing for me to do. However, we are definitely not kids anymore. We hardly know each other now. Oh, and we can't forget about Mark, the *fiancé*. Oh, fuck it to hell! I'm too old to worry about this shit.

Emma

OH MY GOD! What just happened? Cade just took me back 20 years. He used to kiss my forehead all the time when he called me princess. Not in the sarcastic nasty way I might expect from him nowadays, but in a sweet and gentle way. As I got older, when he would do that, I began wanting more. I would always imagine what it would be like to kiss him, I mean *really* kiss him. And now, all these years later, I find myself still trying to imagine the same thing. Oh crap! I'm not going to get any sleep tonight knowing he is in the room right next door!

CHAPTER 8

Emma

I woke up the next day to the sound of my phone going off. When I checked to see who it was, I silenced it. Three missed calls and numerous texts from Mark. Great.

His voicemails and texts started out sweet and progressively got angrier. I knew I needed to talk to him, I owed him that much; I just didn't have anything to say. He let me down. And then there is Caden, who has gotten his whole club involved to help me. I'm just not ready to talk to Mark right now. I'll call him later.

I got up, showered, and got dressed. Now, I'm in need of some coffee. Hopefully they will have some downstairs. I left my room and headed that way. When I made it to the common area of the clubhouse, nobody was around except Honey, who was cleaning up around the bar. Now that I know that she isn't Cade's old lady, it should have been a little easier to talk to her, but I still felt awkward. I reached the bar and said shyly, "Good morning, Honey."

"Morning," she replied. Her short response told me exactly what she thought of me.

"Do you know where I could get a cup of coffee?"

"Coffee is in the kitchen. If you want cream or sugar you will have to find it; me and the boys drink our coffee black and strong." Not the most welcoming response, but really, had I expected anything different? I nodded and headed into the kitchen, where I did find a pot – thankfully still warm – as well as some milk in the fridge.

After I got my coffee, I headed back to the main common room and plopped myself down at the bar. I thought about trying to make conversation with Honey – maybe we could get to know each other better? But in the end I thought better of it and just sat there quietly, drinking my coffee. I really wanted to know where Cade was, but I thought he was a subject that I definitely should not discuss with her.

After I had downed my second cup, Tiny and a couple other members came in. I had never met the other two men, but I knew they were brothers because they wore the same vest that Tiny had on.

"Good morning, Miss Emma," Tiny said, then continued, "Have you met Dbag and Doc?"

"No, I haven't." I looked to the other two men and said, "Nice to meet you, I'm Emma." They both eyed me up and down and smiled. They made me feel a little uncomfortable. "*Are they seriously checking me out?*" I thought to myself. They never said anything to me, just smiled and walked away. After they stepped away, I asked Tiny, "I was wondering – if you are not too busy, would you be able to take me to my apartment? I forgot to pick up my laptop and would really like to get it."

At first, he looked a little nervous. Did I intimidate him that much? But, then he smiled and said, "I'm not sure that's a good idea. Ice told us you were not to leave for any reason."

"Oh, Tiny, it's ok. I told Ice last night that I needed my laptop and he said fine. He knows that I was going to ask you to take me back to my apartment."

Tiny shrugged, "Well, if Ice okayed it, just let me take care of a couple of things and then we can go."

Relieved that I would have my laptop soon I said, "Great. Let me run upstairs to get my purse and I'll be ready to go whenever you are." He nodded and I took my cup to the kitchen and washed it, then went to my room to retrieve my purse and keys. Fifteen minutes later, we left.

We drove to my place in a black pickup truck. I'd wanted to take my car, but Tiny had insisted that that was probably not a good idea and that we should leave my car at the compound.

When we got to my apartment, which was almost 45 minutes away, Tiny waited in the car while I ran up to get my laptop. When I returned, Tiny was talking to another biker who had pulled up next to him on his bike. I recognized him from dinner, but couldn't remember his name. I came down and looked at Tiny, saying, "Thanks, I'm ready to go now." I then looked over to the other biker and said, "Hi, I'm Emma."

He replied, "Nice to meet you, Emma. I'm Spike."

Tiny said, "Prez sent Spike here to check up on you. I guess he isn't too happy that we left the compound." He looked at me with resentment. He hesitated for a moment and then added, "We should head back now. Got everything you need?"

I nodded. I was annoyed that Cade would be upset that I left, especially since he'd said it was ok. Hadn't he? He had. When I get back I am going to make sure he understands that I am not his prisoner. I got in the truck and we headed out, Spike leading the way. We were on the road about 30 minutes when Tiny started to get anxious.

"Tiny, what's wrong?" I asked. He was acting very strange, and he was making me nervous.

"Nothing to worry about, ma'am, Spike and I have this under control." Suddenly I noticed that Spike was not leading the way anymore. He had fallen back and now was behind us. Directly behind him, following very closely, was a black SUV. It was riding really close to him, and I was worried that it would hit him.

"Tiny, what's going on? Why is that SUV following Spike so closely?"

He didn't answer, instead taking a really sharp right turn down a deserted road that was not part of our route back to the clubhouse. He picked up speed, driving rather recklessly, Spike staying close to our tail. At first I thought we had lost the SUV, but then I saw it turn down a side road that we had passed – it was gaining speed on Spike. We were being followed. But why? I thought it best to not engage Tiny in any more conversation and to just let him drive. I'm sure they will explain this all to me when we get back to the clubhouse. If we get back to the clubhouse, that is.

Tiny continued to make a series of twists and turns down the road, turning on various side streets. Soon the black SUV was not in sight, nor was Spike. We eventually came to an alley, and we turned down the alley and waited. We sat there for at least a half hour, just waiting. At this point, my nerves were all but shot. We did not speak, just sat there in silence as Tiny constantly looked out his rearview mirror. Then I heard the roar of a motorcycle and got really scared. But when I turned to see who it was and saw Spike, relief washed over me. Thank God!

Spike walked up to the truck and asked, "You ok, Miss Emma?"

"Yes, thank you. What was that all about?" I asked.

"Club business, ma'am. The less you know the better. The important thing is that you are safe now. Ice would have my ass if I let anything happen to you." Well, that was comforting. He then added, speaking directly to Tiny, "Need to let the boss know. You want me to call him, or do you want to?"

Now even more nervous, Tiny said, "I'm the one that fucked up, I need to call him. If I ever want to get my patch, I need to own this." He pulled out his cell phone and dialed.

"Hey, Ice." He paused and then said, "Yes, I know, I fucked up. I never should have taken her from the compound." Another pause. I could hear Cade yelling, but couldn't make out what he was saying. "We are on our way back now. But, I need to tell you, we ran into some trouble. About thirty minutes from her apartment, we got a tail. I lost them and Spike kept them occupied for a while until they eventually gave up. I'm sorry, boss – this won't happen again." Another pause. Cade was still yelling, even louder now, but I still couldn't understand what he was saying. Tiny said, "I know, I know. It won't happen again. I'll make sure that if she needs something, I go and get it. Yes boss, I understand. She stays put no matter what she tells me." He glanced over to me and gave me a "thanks a lot" look.

Oh no! He's in trouble because of me. But ... Ice did say it was okay. He did! But the more I thought about our conversation last

ICE – KNIGHTS OF SILENCE MC BOOK I

night, I realized he never said anything about me going. He said he would send Tiny. Oh, damn.

When Tiny hung up the phone, he threw it in the console of the truck. I looked over to him and said, "Tiny, I'm so sorry. I didn't know that I was not allowed to leave the clubhouse. I misunderstood him last night when he said he would send you to get it for me. He never said anything about me not going with you. I'm really sorry, Tiny."

"Miss Emma, please do not apologize. Ice is right, I should have known better and offered to go get your laptop for you. I promised him and now I am telling you, it won't happen again."

I still felt bad. Spike was heading back to his bike and we started to back out of the alley. As Tiny was pulling away, he added, "You must be something special to Ice; I've never seen him get that worked up over a woman before."

What could I say to that? Nothing. Which is exactly what I did. We drove the rest of the way to the clubhouse in silence.

CHAPTER 9

Caden - that same day

I was up early this morning. I tossed and turned all night; Emma has got me all tied up in knots. But, there is business to take care of – I have to not think about her and concentrate on my club. Yeah, good luck with that.

We scheduled our meet with Skeeter at 10:30 at Betty's in town. Betty's was a quiet diner, didn't have a big crowd in the mornings, and the people there kept to themselves. It also helped matters that the club owned the diner, so the employees belonged to the Knights. No worries about any of our plans getting in the wrong hands.

Reb, Spike, Ryder, and I got there before Skeeter did. About fifteen minutes after we got settled at a table (all of us getting coffee and Spike a full breakfast), Skeeter arrived. He was a nerdy looking guy, early thirties, tall, with shaggy blond hair and skinny as a rail. I wondered if that boy ever ate anything of substance. But then, when he ordered a huge breakfast, I no longer worried about him eating.

Once we got our coffee and food, I began, "So, Skeeter, as I mentioned on the phone, we need a favor. We've got a situation and we need someone to get inside the Satans' clubhouse and do some snooping around. What do you think about helping us out with something like that?"

Looking nervous, Skeeter replied, "I don't know, Ice. Nobody messes with the Satans. From what I have heard, they are bad news – and if you cross them, unforgiving."

I'd suspected that I would have to convince him. "Yeah, they are," I replied. And then I waited. I let him think for a moment. I've learned from experience that when you need someone to see things your way, sometimes the less you talk the better. Most people don't get this concept and end up talking someone out of what they want him or her to do.

Skeeter asked, "Will I be in danger?"

"I'm not gonna lie to you. Anything that involves the Satans carries with it some element of danger. Like you said, they are unforgiving. But, if you play your cards right, do what we tell you, and mostly keep to yourself, you can be in and out whole in a couple of weeks."

Skeeter looked more nervous. "A couple of weeks! That's a long time, Ice." He looked around at each of us and then added, "I don't know guys, I'm not sure about this."

I'd had a feeling he might be hesitant to help us. After all, he was right; it was dangerous. Normally I wouldn't ask a civilian to do something like this, but Skeeter was our only chance at getting someone we could trust inside. I guess it was time to remind him of what this club has done for him. "Skeeter, I totally get you and understand that what we are asking you to do poses a risk for you. I can't stress enough how much this club needs you right now." I paused for a minute, then added, "Do I need to remind you that this club was there for you when you and your mom needed us?" Skeeter looked up to me, realization on his face. He knew that I wasn't really giving him an option in this. Plain and simple, he owed this club a debt and we were calling it in.

He shrugged, knowing that he didn't have a choice, and said, "So how do I get in?"

Straight to the tough stuff, that's our Skeeter. "Well, we think we have a plan. We've been thinking about setting you up in one of their bars. You'll have to do something that impresses one of the patched members. Haven't figured out that part yet, but my thinking is once you befriend a member, then hopefully you can get in with the club as a hang-around. That way, you will be inside and you can keep your ears and eyes open. Anyone got any ideas?"

Rebel spoke up and said, "How about if we set up a fake ambush on the bar?"

I shook my head. "I don't want any of our boys or Skeeter getting hurt."

Reb jumped in again, "Ice, I don't think you are understanding me. Skeeter can come into the bar, find a patched member, and tell them that he overheard a couple of bikers outside talking about taking down the bar. When they start to ask about the bikers, he can describe our cut. Then, once the Satans are on alert, you know they will head outside. We can then do a drive by, see them all ready to fight and just keep going."

Nodding in agreement, I said, "You might have something there, but this could backfire on us and cause an all-out war with the Satans. If that happens, you all ready for that?" I looked over to Ryder and Spike for their thoughts. Skeeter just sat there and listened.

"I think the plan could work with a bit of fine-tuning," Ryder said. "And about the imminent war? Look man, we have been trying to rid Edinboro of the Satans for a long time. This could be the start of the end for them. This is a chance to get intel on that Brianne chick, but also on the club as well." Ryder looked around to the others for their thoughts. All my guys nodded in agreement.

"Man, this was not how I was expecting this little rescue mission to go, but Ryder is right, we've been dealing with these assholes for a long time. It's time we do something about it." They all agreed and I then added, "We'll need to take this to the table. This isn't a decision that we can make without the input of the whole club. Let's get Skeeter squared away first. So, Ryder, you think it can work?"

"Yeah, I do," he replied. Then he added, "I just think we need to iron out the details."

Spike chimed in and asked, "Hey man, do I get to kill anyone?"

Shaking my head, I replied, "No, no killing. Spike, you know better, there is a civilian involved. Everyone comes out whole."

Spike seemed disappointed, "So you mean I can't kill anyone?"

"No," I replied, "no killing."

Spike shrugged. "It's a good plan. But I would love to kill those sons of bitches!"

Patting him on the back, I replied, "You'll get your chance. When we go in and actually raid the club, I'm sure you will have plenty of opportunities to make your kills."

Skeeter interjected, "Who said anything about killing anyone?"

"Not gonna happen, Skeeter. We'll keep you safe. We know this isn't your war, but we need a civilian to help us get what we need. We just figured you would be perfect. Young guy in awe of the big bad bikers, if you know what I mean."

Skeeter nodded, looking a bit more relaxed. We spent the next hour or so going over the details. Our plan was going into action on Friday, two days from now. This had to work. The last thing I wanted was for Skeeter or one of my boys to get hurt. It just had to work.

After we left the diner, we all headed back to the clubhouse. Once we arrived we all headed for the bar. I knew it was early, but after planning and scheming all morning, we all needed a drink. Looking around the clubhouse, I didn't see Emma anywhere, but Honey was at the bar getting our drinks. "Hey Honey," I called out, "have you seen Emma this morning?"

Looking tired and sullen, she replied, "She came down earlier and got some coffee. Then I saw her leave with Tiny, about 15 minutes ago."

What the fuck! "Where did they go?" Honey shrugged. *What the hell?* She knew she was not supposed to leave here. I can't keep her safe if she isn't here at the clubhouse. I know I may be overreacting and I have no facts yet, but something tells me this whole thing with Brianne has to do with Emma and her association with me. I just can't put my finger on it.

"Ryder, get Tiny on the phone, find out where in the hell he took her, and tell him to get her back here ASAP. And so help me, tell him if anything happens to her on his watch, I'll have his head, not to mention his patch."

"You got it, Ice." Ryder made the call and when he was done he added, "Well boss, it seems that Emma wanted her laptop. Tiny took her back to her apartment and he said that he was bringing her right back."

Nervous about this whole situation, I looked over to Spike and said, "Back them up. I have a bad feeling about this." Spike nodded and headed out.

Fuck this shit. Why did she not stay put? I told her that I would send Tiny over today to get her laptop, but that didn't mean that she was supposed to go with him.

The next couple of hours were pure agony for me. Finally, I got the call from Tiny. I could murder the prospect. What in the hell was he thinking? I'll feel much better when they get back. I kept staring at the door until they finally returned. First came Spike, cool as ever. If I had not sent him, they probably would have gotten run off the road – or worse. Then Tiny came in, looking scared. He should be. I'm not finished with him. Finally, Emma came through the door. They looked like they had been to hell and back. She saw me and headed my way. I got up from the barstool I was sitting on and without thinking pulled her into my arms. The relief of seeing her safe was overwhelming, and all I wanted to do was hold her. I don't know what I would have done if something had happened to her.

"Caden," she squealed, "you are schmooshing me!"

I had to laugh. She used to say that all the time when we were kids. She always asked if I would give her a schmooshing hug.

CHAPTER 10

Caden

"I can't breathe!" Emma said, muffled. Yes, I was still hugging her. If I had my way, I would never let her go. When I finally released her, she stayed so close to me. When she gazed up at me, I could feel that familiar sexual tension that I had felt back when I started to develop different feelings for her. But this time, it was different. I was not the only one experiencing the sexual tension; I could see it on her face. The heat in her eyes was as clear as day. She wanted me!

I couldn't help it. I was so relieved that she was ok, I didn't ask. I wouldn't have been able to wait for a reply anyway. I pulled her against me and crushed my lips to hers. My heart sped up as I tasted those lips for the first time. I couldn't believe it. I was kissing the lips that I had longed to kiss for so many years. My cock got hard and began straining against my jeans, especially when she parted her lips, inviting me in. As I kissed her glorious mouth, her taste started making my head spin. Suddenly, she pulled away, her cheeks flushed, and immediately I felt cold. She stood there for several seconds and then turned and ran to her room.

Fuck! What have I done? I stood there for a minute and looked around, the boys just staring back in shock. Then I heard the kitchen door slam – Honey. I'd deal with that later. Right now I needed to go upstairs and talk to Emma.

As I started to walk away, I turned back to the boys and said, "We will discuss today's ordeal later. Church in an hour. Round everyone up." Then I turned directly to Tiny and said, "I'm not finished with you. Stay put." I turned and headed upstairs.

When I got to Emma's room I could hear her crying, and I immediately opened the door. At this point, knocking was pointless. She was lying on her bed, face down, crying. She used to do that when she was a kid and didn't get her own way, which was not very often. "Emma?" She didn't answer. I waited a couple of seconds and then said again, "Emma?"

Her voice muffled by the bed and her own tears, she yelled, "Go away, Caden!"

"Sweetheart, I'm not going anywhere. We need to talk about what just happened." I went into the bathroom and grabbed the roll of toilet paper, and then sat on the bed next to her. "Here," I said, handing her the toilet paper. "Dry your eyes and talk to me. Why are you so upset?"

She sat up and grabbed the toilet paper from my hand. Pulling off a sheet, she dried her eyes and blew her nose. She still didn't speak, and I felt that a little more coaxing would help. "Emma, sweetheart, we need to talk about this. Since when have you ever not been able to talk to me about anything that's bothering you?" I nudged her and she smiled shyly.

Then, she looked at me, eyes swollen, and said, "Caden, I can't. I can't do this now. Please don't make me." She sounded just like she had when she was a child. Part of me didn't have the heart to push her, but I was not about to let this go another minute. Something very intense happened between us downstairs and we needed to get to the bottom of it.

I leaned into her, wrapping my arm around her shoulder and pulling her close. She started to cry again. "Emma, why are you crying?"

Muffled, she said, "I can't tell you." Ok, now she really sounded like a child. At this rate, we would never get anything settled between us – and I have church in an hour.

"We need to talk about this now. I have a meeting in less than an hour, and I will not leave things with you unsettled. So, why don't I start … I kissed you. You kissed me back. I'm not gonna say I'm sorry, because I am not. I have wanted to taste those luscious lips of yours for a very long time." There, I said it, now I am just waiting for all hell to break loose. Hearing her tell me again how much she hates me will just be the icing on the cake of this shitty day.

She sniffled a couple of times and then said, "You have?" Now that was not what I was expecting – I was expecting her to yell.

I brushed my thumb over her cheek and wiped away a tear. I said, "Yes, I have. Does that bother you?"

She turned away and got up from the bed. She started pacing and then said, "I am not going to do this now. I can't."

I got up and walked over to her, placing my hands on her shoulders to stop her pacing. With her facing me, I said, "Look at me." She would not. "Emma, I mean it. If I am going to tell you everything, you will look at me when I do." She hesitantly looked up and I continued, "Did you really think that all those times that I pushed you away was because I didn't want to be around you? Or that I stopped caring about you?" She nodded. "Well, you are wrong. I pushed you away 'cause I was developing feelings for you that I should not have been feeling. You were a teenager and I was an adult. It was not right. But, it seemed the more I pushed you away, the more you came back, until the day you came to the clubhouse. Emma, I knew you were coming. I set that whole thing up so you would stop once and for all and I would not be tempted to take advantage of you."

She looked confused and asked, "But Caden, why? You were so mean and hateful to me that day. And how did you know I would come to the clubhouse?"

"It was all an act. I meant none of it. I knew you were coming because you texted me."

"But you said you never got my text."

"I lied." So now she knew the truth. This could go two ways. Either she could really hate me, and that would be the end for me … or, she could realize how I feel about her and run into my arms. Holding my breath, I waited for her to say something. Anything.

"But that girl, you were still with her." Again, that was not what I was expecting.

"Yes, I was. I'll be honest with you; I've been with a lot of women. Just because I couldn't have you, doesn't mean that I have gone without. But, none of them were you."

Quietly, she asked, "Honey?"

Fuck, I didn't want to get into specifics with her ... but I am not going to lie to her again. "Yes, including Honey."

"I thought so." She turned and sat back down on the bed. "Caden, I know you are looking at me for some type of reaction to all this, but right now I feel nothing. I'm numb. I need time to sort this through, and you have a meeting to go to. Just leave. We can talk about this later."

Well, I guess I was wrong. There was a third option on how that conversation would go. I'm not sure I like this one, but at least she isn't telling me she hates me. Realizing that it was best to do as she asked, I quietly left the room and headed down to the chapel for my meeting.

CHAPTER 11

Emma

After Caden left, my head was spinning. All these years I had believed that he didn't want me. I was sure that he would never be interested in me in that way, especially with all the women that he had available to him. I know how women are drawn to bikers; I saw it firsthand with Brianne. I always told myself that I would never be one of those girls that hangs with bikers. But if I'm honest with myself, I am definitely one of those girls – just one that is only interested in one biker.

Realization of what just happened finally hit me: OMG! He kissed me!! I can't believe it. He finally kissed me. I swear I thought I was going to melt into him. My heart was beating so fast and loud, I'm sure he could hear it. And the kiss hadn't been sloppy like Mark's kisses; it was hot and passionate. His tongue was soft and controlled. Our lips moved together as if we were in a very well-choreographed dance, just like I always imagined it. All of a sudden I felt giddy.

He lied to me. He hurt me so badly; I should hate him. I should leave right now and never turn back. But I can't. I love him. Does he feel the same? I doubt it. I'm sure his feelings are more lustful than loving.

Just then my phone began to ring. I looked over at the display; it was Mark, again. I let it ring a couple of times and answered it. "Hello."

"Emma, what the hell is going on? I've been trying to reach you since yesterday."

Well, good to talk to you, too. Why does he always have to start a conversation like that, yelling at me for one reason or another? Out loud I said, "I'm sorry, Mark. I told you in my text, I just needed time."

"Time for what, Emma? I thought we settled everything when you agreed to marry me."

So, do I tell him now or just string him along? If I sever this relationship now, then I will be free to explore what is happening with Caden. But, is it fair to do this over the phone? On the other hand, I don't know when I'll be able to leave here, and I can't handle getting phone calls like this every day. "Mark, I think ..."

Before I could finish, he interrupted me and said, "Why were you at the apartment today? I thought you left town."

What?? How did he know I was at the apartment today? He was at work, so I know he could not have been there this morning. "How did you know I was at the apartment today? Are you following me?"

He stuttered and said, "O-Of course not. Why would I follow you? That's ridiculous. I was going to meet a client and happened to drive past. I saw a black pickup truck parked outside, and a guy on a motorcycle out front. I was sure that they were not there to see you, but then you came out and got in the truck. What is going on, Emma? Did you go to the Knights? Is that who you are shacking up with now?"

Ok, now I was pissed. He is spying on me. "You know what, Mark? Where I am and what I am doing is none of your business. This engagement is officially over. I didn't want to do this over the phone, but you are being such an ass. I don't need this right now."

I should have just hung up at that point. That was my first mistake. He was silent for a minute and then yelled into the phone, "What the fuck, Emma?! You can't break our engagement!"

"I'm sorry, Mark, but I just did."

"Well you little bitch. You can't get rid of me that easy. You and I are meant to be together. You don't realize what you just did, the fate you have cast on the ones you love. You'll be sorry, and you'll come running back to me." Then he hung up.

Well, if I had been unsure about any decisions that I have made in the last twenty-four hours, I was not anymore. My conversation with Mark definitely convinced me that he has changed. I don't know what has changed him, but I am certain that he is not the man I want to spend the rest of my life with. And what was he talking about when he said "the ones I love"? Could he have something to do with Brianne? Could that be why he wouldn't help me find her? No, no, no, I refuse to believe it. It can't be.

It was all too much. Brianne missing, staying here, being followed this morning, Mark and Caden … it was just too much. I needed to get out of here, but I knew if I left someone else would get in trouble because of me. I needed a drink. That's it. I was not a drinker, but right then a warm shot of whiskey sounded very enticing.

I left my room and headed downstairs to the bar. All the guys were gone except for Tiny and the bartender from last night – I couldn't remember his name. Honey was also standing behind the bar. Oh great; just what I needed right now. My need for that drink overpowered my distaste for Honey, so I marched myself right up to that bar. Honey ignored me and continued wiping the bar down. She had several shot glasses lined up on the counter as if she was expecting a big crowd. "Excuse me?" Nothing. Not even a glance my way. So I decided to just ask her. "Honey, may I please have a shot of whiskey?"

Shocked by my request, she finally acknowledged me. "Coming right up." As Honey was placing my drink on the bar in front of, one of the doors across the room opened up and an array of bikers emerged. They all headed straight for the bar – I felt as if I was being bombarded by leather. The last one out of the room was Cade. He paused at the door and scanned the room. When he spotted me, he made a beeline right for me.

"What are you drinking?" he asked with a smile.

CHAPTER 12

Caden

When I arrived at our meet, all the boys were waiting. "Alright boys, let's get this shit settled. Appreciate you all getting here so quickly. We had a problem today that I think may be related to Emma and her friend." I looked over at Tiny and gave him the look that said, *"This is all your fault, fucker."* I tried not to be so harsh on him; after all, it was his quick reflexes that helped them get away. But Emma should not have been in that position in the first place, and for that, he was totally to blame. "For those of you who were not involved, Tiny took Emma to her apartment today. When they left, they got a tail. Black SUV, plate #CXY1952." I looked to Dbag and said, "Get an ID on that as soon as we're done here."

Grabbing his pen, he jotted down the number and said, "Right boss, I'm on it."

I then continued, "Tiny and Spike were able to lose the tail and everyone returned whole. I feel that there is more to this missing girl situation, but I just can't get all the pieces together to make sense. Hopefully once Skeeter gets inside we will have more answers."

Doc spoke up and said, "How did the meet with Skeeter go?"

"Good. We decided that he needed to make friends with the Satans. You know, do something that will make them indebted to him. So, Friday night, he is going to Dirty Dick's. As you all know, that's the Satans' off-compound hangout, especially on Fridays.

He's gonna befriend a patched member and tell them that he overheard two guys outside on bikes talking about raiding the bar. It will be enough for them to at least check it out. When they get up to check it out, he will text Rebel. We will be waiting down the road. When they come out, we will do a drive by so that they can see Skeeter was telling them the truth. Boom, the Satans have a new best friend."

"Ice, are we declaring war on the Satans?" Doc asked.

"Well, that was the next topic up for discussion. We realize that if Skeeter tells them that he overheard us talking about taking down their bar, they will definitely look at it as an act of war. You all ready for that?"

Chig chimed in, "Those motherfuckers killed Red, Ace, and several other brothers. We got some retribution for Red and Ace, but those fuckers still need to go down."

"Yeah, let's get rid of them once and for all," Dbag added.

Looking around the room, it was clear everyone was in agreement. "All those in favor of moving forward with the Skeeter plan, knowing this could ultimately cause a war between the Knights and the Satans, say I." It was unanimous. "Ok, now that that's settled, what do you all think about the plan for Skeeter?"

"I like it. Gets him in fast," Doc said.

"I think we can take eight guys. I don't care who all goes, but Reb, Hawk, and Spike, plan to be there." The guys discussed it amongst themselves and it was decided that along with myself, Rebel, Hawk, Spike, that Doc, Chigger, Ryder, and Weasel would perform the drive by. When the Skeeter business was finished, I asked, "Any other business?" The guys looked around, shaking their heads. "We're done then. Thanks again, boys." The meeting dispersed and the guys headed out the door. However, I lingered behind. I needed to gather my thoughts. I was about to face Emma again and settle this business between us, and I couldn't do that unprepared.

When I finally left the room, I scanned the clubhouse for Emma. She was at the bar, with a shot in her hand. What the fuck? It's only two in the afternoon. That was not like her. I walked directly in her direction. When I got to the bar, I asked, "What are you drinking?"

Emma

I picked up my shot and downed it, slammed the glass on the bar, turned toward Cade and said, "Whiskey." Then I looked over to Honey and said, "I'll have another one." She nodded.

Caden said, "No! She will not have another one, Honey." She immediately stopped pouring my drink. What is his problem?

"Cade, I want another drink!" I said sternly. Who in the hell does he think he is? He can't tell me what I can or can't do. When Cade saw the defiance in my eyes, he knew he had lost this round. Yes, some things never change. Cade nodded to Honey and she finished pouring my drink and brought it over. I picked up my second shot and downed it, again slamming the glass down on the bar.

"Holy shit, Emma. I never knew you drank the hard stuff." He seemed surprised, and acted as if he was proud of me for some reason. Maybe I just proved to him that I could hang with the big boys. Who am I kidding? It takes more than downing a shot to run with these guys. He continued, "Why are you drinking?"

Defiant, I replied, "I can drink if I want to. I'm a grown woman, Cade. I'm not a child anymore." Where did that come from? Suddenly, I was angry. He was not my father or my keeper … he reminded me of Mark. Aaggh! Men!

"Calm down there, sweetheart, I was just asking. It's not like you to be drinking hard liquor in the middle of the afternoon."

"How would you know what is like me? You haven't seen or spoken to me in eleven years. I've changed, Cade. There are a lot of things I do now that I didn't do before. Get used to it." Damn, I was being a bitch. I know this was all stemming from my argument with Mark and I was taking it out on Caden, but he deserved it. In the last 24 hours he has managed to tie my emotions up into several knots. It was making me crazy.

"Emma! Stop! Now!" he said. He was mad. Well hell, he made me mad, too. But then he gave me that look – you know, that one look that your parents gave you as a kid that says, "If you don't stop now, I'm gonna take you over my knee." I immediately refrained from saying anything more. I figured it was best at this point to discuss my anger with him in private instead of in front of his entire club.

CHAPTER 13

Caden

Emma was pushing my buttons, but I could not allow her to disrespect me like that in front of my boys. Luckily for her she got the hint and shut up. She asked Honey for another shot, downed it, and then left the bar, heading toward her room. I imagine she is going to be feeling pretty good in about fifteen minutes when she starts to experience the effects of the three shots of whiskey she just consumed. I had to laugh to myself. I'd never seen Emma drunk. My guess is that I was about to.

Right after Emma left, Dbag came out of the back room. "Ice, got an ID on that black SUV." Shit, that was fast. He is so good at this shit.

"Whatcha got?"

"SUV is registered to a Mark Grayson. He's a big-time attorney, works in Erie. Lives here in Edinboro." Holy fucking shit. Could this be a coincidence? Not likely. In my experience, there are no coincidences. So, why was Mark following Emma?

"You got anything else?"

"Well, I think I might have found something, but I don't know. I searched both the DMV databases and the crime databases. An incident report showed up about the chick's disappearance. Emma's friend."

I looked at him surprised. "What?" *What the fuck is going on?*

"Well, apparently, the same black SUV was noted on the report. There weren't any details as to how or why it was there. It was just arbitrarily listed on the report as a vehicle involved, but with no evidence tying the SUV to her disappearance. I'm not sure, boss, I've never seen a police report like this one before."

Could this be a coincidence, or was there more about Mr. Grayson that I didn't know? Fuck, now I have not only this situation with Emma's friend, but now her fiancé. My gut told me that there was some type of link between Grayson and Brianne, but I just couldn't put my finger on it. Something with all of this was just not settling well with me. If Grayson was involved, that would explain why that SOB would not help her. I shook my head. No, I was jumping to conclusions. I needed to get more facts before I place blame. Even though nothing would give me more pleasure than to nail that cocksucker to the wall for this.

"Dbag, I want you to find out everything you can on Mark Grayson. And when I say everything, I mean everything! I want to know how many times he pisses in a day! You got me?"

"Yes sir!" That kid loved this shit. He quickly headed back to the office to start digging. Next I needed to find out what Emma was not telling me. Perhaps she could shed some light on this. I was pissed and angry. The thought of Grayson being involved in this made my blood boil; however, I had to remember to keep my cool with Emma or I wouldn't get anything from her.

I walked upstairs to her room. The door was closed, so I knocked. No answer. I knocked again: still no answer. I was starting to get worried, so I opened the door. Emma was passed out on the bed. Served her right for drinking like that. I decided to let her sleep. I wasn't going to get any coherent answers from her in that state. I would wait until she sobered up.

I went back downstairs and decided that I needed a drink. I walked up to the bar and Honey asked, "What'll you have, Ice?"

"The usual, please." She grabbed my bottled of Maker's and poured me a drink. The bourbon was smooth going down with only the slightest burn. After the day I was having, the warmth in my chest felt good. I needed Emma to sober up fast. I was sure she had some information that would help me figure out what was going on with all of this shit. Part of me didn't think that this was solely a rival MC issue. What kind of guy has she gotten herself mixed up with? Last night I was beginning to feel that I was overreacting in keeping her here, but after today – the tail, and the news about Grayson – I know now that I did the right thing. I asked Honey for another drink.

When she brought it over, she asked, "You look troubled. Is there anything I can do for you?"

"Naw, sweetheart, I'm good. Just got a lot on my mind."

After a few minutes went by, the other brothers that had been lingering around the bar dispersed and Honey and I were alone at the bar. "Ice, can we talk?" Fuck, I did not need this right now. But I'm not a total ass. She deserved to know the truth about us. Christ knows, I hadn't been fair to her.

I shrugged and said, "Why don't you take a break. We can talk in my office." She smiled, finished putting some of the bottles away, and then followed me to my office.

When we got there, she was the last one in and closed the door behind her. As soon as we were completely alone, she ran into my arms. "Ice, I've missed you so much." I tried to push her away, but she was holding on to me so tight … I figured I would let her have a minute. When she started to ease up her grip, I eased her out of my embrace.

She looked up to me, confused. "What's wrong?"

"Honey, I'm sorry, but I can't. We had fun, but it's over."

Tears welled up in her eyes. "But why?" she asked.

"Honey, I'm sure you knew this was coming," I stated matter-of-factly.

"But, Ice, I thought …" She didn't finish. She knew. I knew she'd been hoping that things would change and I would make her my old lady, but that was never going to happen. Not when my heart always belonged to Emma. And especially not now when Emma and I had reconnected. I was not about to jeopardize that right now. No way.

"Honey, Emma and I have a history. I need to see where this – whatever this is between us – is gonna go. I'm sorry if I hurt you. It was never my intent. But you knew from the beginning I was not in the market for an old lady."

Sullen, she nodded. "I know, I was just hoping ... well, that maybe ... oh, never mind." She turned toward the door, and then looked back at me and said, "We had fun though, didn't we?"

I smiled, "We sure did." As she opened the door I called out, "Honey, you know you always have a home here. You take care of my boys and me like nobody else. If that's what you want, that will never change."

"Thanks, Ice. That means a lot to me." She turned again to leave and then added quietly, "I hope things work out for you and Emma. You deserve to be happy."

"Thanks, Honey. I hope you find some happiness too." She left.

Whew! That went a lot easier than I thought. I really hated hurting her. She was a good woman and would do anything for this club. She was loyal to the core. However, what it all came down to was that she was not Emma. It's always been Emma.

CHAPTER 14

Caden

About an hour after Honey left my office, I heard a knock at my door. "Come in." Dbag came through the door, looking as if he was the cat that swallowed the canary. "You got intel on Grayson?"

"I do, and you ain't gonna like it."

Fuck, could this day get any worse? "What'd you get?"

"As I told you before, Grayson is an attorney. He's a senior partner in the firm of Grayson, Grayson, and Grayson in Erie. He's the second Grayson. 90% of his cases are thugs that he has gotten off; he's famous for it. But the kicker ... his number one paying client ... Satans Rebels MC."

Holy fuck. He was right, I didn't like it. "What else?"

Dbag continued, "Well, the guy is loaded, possessive, and has anger issues. Daddy, who is the first Grayson, has gotten him off on several assault charges against women in the past. I heard that one of the ladies was pregnant. He threw her down a flight of stairs because he thought she was cheating on him. She lost the baby and is living out her days in a mental institution in New York. I guess it really fucked up her head."

"Damn! Emma is engaged to this guy, Dbag. What is she thinking, hooking up with a bastard like that? Do you think that he had something to do with Brianne?"

"I'm afraid so, Prez. All the signs point in that direction. My guess is that he did something and the MC is covering for him."

"Fuck! This is not good. I need to talk to Emma now. This can't wait." I strode out, leaving Dbag standing in my office. Damn, I didn't even thank him. But I had to take care of business.

When I got to Emma's room, the door was open and she was nowhere to be found. Shit. Where in the hell was she? I went back downstairs and scanned the clubhouse. No sign of her. So help me, if she left this compound again, I'll put her over my knee and spank her ass! I headed for the kitchen, and to my surprise, found her having a cup of coffee with Honey. Oh shit, I sure as hell don't need this.

"Emma, I need to talk to you," I said.

"Cade, can it wait, please? I've got a splitting headache and would love to finish my coffee."

"Nope, can't wait. Bring your coffee. My office, now!" I was more stern than normal, but I needed answers and I needed them now.

As I walked out of the kitchen, I overheard Honey say, "Emma, you better go. Ice isn't used to waiting for anyone." By the time I got to my office, Emma was trailing behind slowly. That's my good girl. I was not in the mood to deal with her independence.

I waited for her to come into the office and then I closed the door.

"Caden, what's wrong?"

"I don't know, Emma, why don't you tell me?"

Confused, she answered, "I have no idea what you are talking about."

"Ok, how about I start. Why don't you tell me about Mark Grayson?"

Still confused, she said, "Cade, I told you about Mark. He was my fiancé."

Was? Did I miss something?? My head was spinning. There was already too much info in my brain to think straight, and then she drops this bomb on me. When did things change?

"Caden, please tell me what is going on. You're scaring me."

"You need to sit down." When Emma seated herself I continued, "We found out some information about your Mr. Grayson today."

"Why would you be looking into Mark?" she asked quizzically. I could still see the confusion on her face. I was trying to lay this on her easy; I knew she would freak when she found out that Mark was the one following her.

"Emma, Grayson was the one tailing you and Tiny today." She looked up at me, but didn't say anything. Not the reaction I was expecting. I reiterated what I had said, "Emma, did you hear me? It was Grayson."

She didn't seem surprised. What the hell? There is more to this than she has told me. "Damnit Emma, say something."

After a few seconds, she finally spoke up. "I had a feeling it was Mark. Especially after our phone call today."

What. The. Fuck! "You better start talking now. And I mean it, you better tell me everything!"

She began to fidget in her chair. I'm sure she was hoping I would cut her some slack. No way in hell. She was gonna spill everything. "Where do you want me to start?"

I knew there was more to this than met the eye. Shit! "How about from the beginning? That's always a good place to start."

She began, "I met Brianne in college. She was my roommate. We hit it off so well together, we remained roomies until we both graduated. When I met Brianne, she was dating Mark – that's how I met him. They had only been dating for a few months before things suddenly ended between them. I never knew all the details of their breakup. Brianne never talked about it, and I never asked or pushed her. I got the impression that he was not the love of her life."

She took a couple of deep breaths and then continued, "Three years after we graduated we ran into Mark in a bar. Brianne was well over him and was dating someone else at the time. When he started hanging around us, I thought he was trying to get Brianne back. But, it was me he was pursuing. I did not feel comfortable with his intentions. You know, the 'friend code' and all."

I looked at her quizzically, but I knew better than to ask. Realizing that I didn't have a clue what she meant by the "friend code", she continued, "Girlfriends have a code: you don't date your friend's ex-boyfriend. But Brianne encouraged me. She wanted me to date Mark. So, after several weeks of him pursuing me, I finally agreed to go out with him."

I was getting frustrated, as I was not sure how all this pertained to the issue at hand. "Emma, I assume you have a point?"

"I do, Cade – just be patient, please. I think this back history is important. I've been thinking about this and it is all making sense now." She took another deep breath, as if she was about to head into battle, and then continued, "So, Mark and I started dating. At first, he was quite charming. Our relationship blossomed, and over the last several years, we talked more and more about marriage. However, the more we talked about it, the more afraid of marrying him I was. I kept putting him off. Something was always holding me back, but I couldn't put my finger on it.

"Three days before Brianne disappeared she told me that she was wrong about Mark. She said that she didn't have time to tell me everything, but that I needed to break all ties with him. At that point, I really didn't know what to think. I had been with Mark for the last five years. So, I did the only thing that made sense at the time. I questioned him." She started to fidget again and I could see she was getting nervous about what she was going to say next.

"When I confronted Mark, he became irate. He basically turned the conversation back on me, saying that I didn't believe in him nor trust him. He could not believe that I would even consider something that Brianne had said about him to be true. I had a hard time coming to terms with his anger, but I chalked it up to him having a bad day. Three days later, Brianne disappeared. When I asked Mark for help, he became angry again. So, here I am. That's why I came to you."

I sat there for several minutes, taking in all that she had said. "Ok, so now why don't you tell me about the phone call today?"

"When I left yesterday, I could not bring myself to talk to Mark. I was afraid he would be angry, and frankly he scared me when he got angry. So I texted him. Told him I needed to get away for a few days. I didn't tell him where I was going or what I was doing. Ever since then, he has been blowing up my phone. He has been calling and texting non-stop. I kept ignoring his calls and texts. Today, I realized that I needed to talk to him, so I finally answered his call. When I did, he became irate. He knew that I had gone to the apartment. He knew who I was with. How would he know those things if he was not tailing me? I realized that this relationship was never going to work. So, I broke off our engagement. When I did, he changed. He spoke to me as if I was dirt on the side of the road. And, he threatened me." She stopped talking to allow me to absorb that last statement.

"He what?" My blood pressure was rising by the minute. When I got my hands on that prick …

"He threatened me." She was trying to keep me calm, but it was not working.

"Emma, what exactly did he say?" I said, trying very hard to keep my composure.

"Well … he called me a bitch. That's not normal for him. He has never spoken to me like that before. He said that I can't get rid of him that easy, that we are meant to be together. But then he said something that really scared me. He said that I didn't realize the fate I had cast on the ones I love. He said I would be sorry and that he was sure I would come running back to him." She paused for a moment. Then she added, "Maybe now you can understand why I was drinking earlier."

I couldn't believe what I was hearing. That fucking son of a bitch; what a cocksucker! I'm gonna kill him. It all made sense now. "Emma, you are safe here. I will not let him or anyone else harm you." I knelt down in front of her and made her look at me. "Do you believe me?" She nodded. I then asked, "Do you trust me?"

She nodded again as tears started to well up in her eyes. "What about Brianne? Caden, what if he has done something to her?"

"Right now, I don't know. But we will figure this out, I promise." I needed to talk to Skeeter, give him a description of Grayson. Maybe if he sees him hanging around the Satans, we can find Brianne. "Emma, why don't you go and get some dinner. I have a few things I need to take care of. I'll join you later. I think spaghetti is on the menu." I winked at her, knowing that spaghetti is her absolute favorite thing to eat.

"Spaghetti!" she squealed. Damn, I know her so well. She left my office and I called Skeeter and filled him in on the details.

CHAPTER 15

Emma

That was the best spaghetti I had ever eaten. Honey sure could cook. She was being a lot nicer to me, too. I wonder what was up with that? I wasn't complaining, just curious.

I finished my dinner and realized that I hadn't seen Caden all night ... he didn't even come down to eat. I was sure he was busy, and this whole situation had us both on edge, but he has to eat. Maybe I should take him a plate? I leaned over to Honey, who was sitting next to me, and asked, "Do you think we should take Caden – oh, I mean Ice – some dinner?"

She smiled and said, "I've already sent a plate to his office for him, although I doubt he will touch it. When he is engrossed in work, he never eats." Suddenly, I was jealous of her all over again. I hated that fact that she knew more about him now than I did. All I had was our memories, but she knew the man he was today. I hated that. Still, I had nobody to blame for that except myself. He may have pushed me away, but I chose to stay away. Well, hopefully I can make up for lost time.

I helped Honey clean up, although she protested. I wanted us to be friends and I was trying; I could see she was, too. After we cleaned up, Cade still had not emerged from his office. I decided it was best to just retire for the night. It had been a long day and I was exhausted.

I got a cup of decaf coffee, asked Scratch to drop a shot of whiskey in it, and took it upstairs with me. If I had any trouble sleeping, I was sure the drink would help.

Once I got to my room I did my normal bedtime routine; you know, wash my face, brush my teeth, etc. When I was done, I couldn't fall asleep. I sipped at my coffee and decided to do some work instead.

I had totally lost track of time when I heard a knock at the door. It was quiet, and then I heard Cade call softly, "Emma? Are you still awake?" I looked over at my phone lying on the nightstand: it was 1:48 am. Why was Cade still awake? Actually, why was I still awake?

"Come in, Caden. I'm still awake." He walked into to my room, looking exhausted. I don't think I have ever seen him so worn down, not even when his parents passed away. I was beginning to worry about him. "Caden, are you ok? You look like you have been to hell and back."

"I'm good, sweetheart. Just trying to get things in order for tomorrow. We have to play this right or we may never find Brianne, or figure out why Grayson is involved with this. But don't go worrying your pretty little head about that; just trust that I got you."

"Cade, can I ask you something?" I already knew the answer, but I just needed his reassurance … to make it real.

"Sure, what's up?"

"This thing … this thing that you are doing for me, the plans you are making to find Brianne, is there a possibility that you or your brothers could get hurt?" I just had to know.

He nodded. "I'm not going to sugarcoat it for you. There is a good possibility that we could get hurt. But Emma, you have to understand, this is what we do. We won't back out of a fight just because we might get hurt."

Since I had come here, I had felt this was dangerous. I guess deep down I'd known it would be. But hearing Cade say it made it real. "Promise you will be careful? I've waited a long time to get you back in my life, I can't lose you now."

He walked over to the bed, leaned over, and kissed my forehead. "Beautiful, you can count on that. You are stuck with me. I know we have a lot to talk about, but right now, my brain hurts. Why don't you slide over, put that laptop away, and show your man how much you love him?"

What in the world is he talking about, my man? "Since when did you become my man?"

"About twelve hours ago, sweetheart, when I kissed you and you kissed me back." Suddenly I felt giddy. Caden and I were finally together, if that's what we were. There were so many unanswered questions between us, but just then, I agreed with him. My brain hurt too. All I wanted to do was snuggle up against "my man".

Following his instruction, I closed my laptop and tucked it away in the case lying next to the bed. When I looked up, Cade was standing next to the bed in nothing but a pair of black boxer briefs. Oh my God! He was magnificent! He was so different now. I remembered a tall, lanky, and scrawny boy. The Caden that was standing before me was a tall, muscular man with chiseled abs and downright sexy tattoos. And please do not get me started on the V! You know, that incredible part of a man's body where his lower abs meet his hip. He was beautiful, and I couldn't stop staring at him. He looked over at me and caught me staring. He grinned and sauntered toward me, then pulled me from the bed and into his arms. He held me close, and his body felt so good against me. He slowly nuzzled my neck and whispered in my ear, "Fuck, you smell so good." He held me like that and took a deep breath against my ear. There were goosebumps all over my body. I could feel the moisture pooling between my legs. Oh dear God, I wanted him. I didn't want to wait, I wanted him right now!

Caden turned me around and wrapped his arms around me. His body pressed flush up against me, with my back to his front. He held me with his left hand, pulling me even closer against his body. His left hand was splayed across my stomach while his right hand was pulling my hair away from my ear. He pressed his lips to my ear and said with a ragged breath, "So tell me, beautiful, did you end your engagement with that asshole?"

My legs were quivering from his words and breathlessly I answered, "Yes."

His left hand moved up my stomach, pulling my tank top with it. With the edge of his thumb, he gently stroked the underside of my breast. I began to tremble – if he wasn't holding me, I probably wouldn't have been able to stand. His touch felt so good. He slid his hand higher up my body, tracing over my ribs until he had the full weight of my breast in his palm. He feathered kisses down my neck. He took his right hand and began to slide it down my front to the waistband of my shorts. He hesitated for a brief moment, as if he was asking me for permission. Then he whispered, "Emma, if you don't want this, stop me. If you don't stop me now and I keep going, I won't be able to stop later if you change your mind."

"Then don't," I whispered. I didn't want to stop him. I couldn't if I tried. I'd wanted this for as long as I could remember. I needed him, and by the bulge that was pressing into my backside, I knew he needed me too.

I was so desperate for him and wanted him to kiss me. I needed to feel his lips fused with my own. I leaned back, hoping that he would get the hint. He did. No hesitation, no questions asked, he claimed my lips with a need like I have never known. Before I knew it, his hand moved back to my hips and he was lifting me toward the wall, bracing me between the wall and his chest. His hardness was pressing against my behind and the pleasure was unbearable. He was tormenting me with his lips and his hands. Breathlessly, I whispered, "Caden, I want you." When he continued with his torture, I begged, "Please." With my final plea, he pulled me away from the wall and carried me to the bed. He tossed me upon the rumpled covers of the bed and immediately reached for the band around my shorts and started to tug.

He then hesitated and looked up at me and asked, "Are you sure?" He looked worried. Did he really think I would push him this far and then change my mind? Obviously, he had no idea how long I have wanted this.

Anxious with anticipation, I nodded reassuringly. "Yes, I'm sure."

Convinced, Caden quickly removed my shorts and my tank top. He drew my hand down to his boxers and pressed my palm against his erection. "Touch me. I need to feel your touch Emma, please." I hesitated, but only for a second – not because I didn't want this, but more because I was unsure as to where this all would go. Sure, it was clear he wanted me then, but would he want me tomorrow? I loved him so much, at least the Caden that I had known all my life. He's different now and a little intimidating by the power that he holds. However, the temptation to touch him was too strong. Trembling, my hand slid down the inside of his boxers. Caden groaned as he jerked his hips, thrusting into my palm. Twenty years ago he had been a teenage boy that I had a crush on. Now, he was this beautiful man that I knew I would never be able to get enough of. I ran my other hand over his chest, broad and thick with muscle, tracing the intricate tattoos that covered his entire chest. My right hand continued to stroke his huge cock, as it lay heavy in my hand. Caden relished in the pleasure that I was giving him.

He bent down and took my nipple between his lips. He sent shivers of need to my core as he rolled it with his tongue, feeling the combination of the cool air on my skin coupled with his hot, wet mouth. I couldn't help the moan that escaped, and the instinctive arch to my back offered him more. He released my nipple and said, "That's right, baby. Give it to me. Give it all to me." He then turned his attention to my other breast. He placed his hands on my hips and I ground the curve of my sex against his thigh. The friction felt amazing and my body was enflamed with need. I continued to rock against him, never getting enough; I needed more than the tease of him against me that he was allowing me to have. I tightened my grip on his shaft and worked him as hard as I dared. I slid my hand up and down his shaft, being sure to touch him from balls to tip in a steady rhythm. He gave out a tortured groan, and demanded, "Harder." I didn't think I could get much wetter, but hearing the want and need in his voice, I realized that I was wrong. He just made me want him more.

"Caden, please, I can't take this torture anymore. Take me. Now."

"Are you ready for me?" he asked breathlessly.

"Touch me, and find out for yourself." With my words, Caden palmed my cleft and slid his fingers through my folds. He groaned as he pushed one finger inside. I immediately clenched around him.

"Oh God baby, you are so hot. So wet. So ready." He got up from the bed, walked over to his jeans and pulled out his wallet. Digging through, he pulled out a condom and quickly removed the wrapper and sheathed himself. "There's no turning back now, Emma. If we go any further, I own you. All of you," he stated. He waited for a brief moment and then asked, "Do you understand what I mean?" I nodded and then he asked, "Do you accept these terms?"

I really wasn't sure what he meant, but conversation was the last thing I wanted right then. All I wanted at that point was him. I didn't care what he was asking, I was primed and ready to accept any terms he was offering. I quickly nodded. My body ached for him, and in all honestly, my brain was not making any rational thoughts. All I wanted was to feel his hot hardness inside me. Caden walked over to the bed and positioned himself on top of me. He entered me with one powerful thrust and then stopped. The only movement was his body shaking, and I could sense that he was trying to hold back. He was huge, and I know that he was waiting patiently for me to adjust to his size. I didn't know if I could take any more, but I wanted more. His cock was throbbing inside of me. I pushed against him, encouraging him to take me deeper, harder. I whispered, "You feel so good, Caden, so hard, so thick."

"Emma," he said breathlessly. He groaned, and with a sense of purpose started to hammer into me. My hands dug into his flesh as I tried to keep up with the frantic rhythm of his thrusts. He was so deep, and I could feel every movement of his hardness inside me. This was nothing like I imagined. I had dreamed about being with Caden for so many years, but I never imagined this kind of passion and the burning need that I feel for him. We were both sweaty as our bodies slammed together, the sound of our flesh slapping against each other. It was incredibly erotic and my orgasm built quickly, heating my body even more. My muscles coiled inside and out, and I felt as if I was going to combust. My undoing came when

Caden reached between us and brushed his thumb against my clit. I exploded with a low, guttural groan, shuddering around him. It was too intense, but Cade continued to hammer into me. I could feel his muscles become taut and I could see the sweat beading on his brow. As he continued to find his release, I could feel another orgasm building. I could feel Caden growing inside me and just as he reached his climax, I did too. This orgasm tore through us both as we rode it out together. When the last ripple of pleasure had faded away, he collapsed on top of me. He lay there for several minutes and then finally he released me and rolled to my side. He pulled me to his chest. As he held me, he murmured in my ear, "My beautiful Emma."

We lay there for several minutes and eventually I could hear Caden's steady breathing. He was asleep. It wasn't long after that I found sleep myself, realizing that my only dream had just come true.

When I woke the next morning, Caden was gone.

CHAPTER 16

Caden

I woke up around 5 am, a little confused as to my surroundings. Then glancing over, I saw Emma lying next to me. She looked so damn sexy, lying there with only the sheet to cover her. My beautiful Emma. Finally. If I didn't have shit to do today, I would wake her ass up and take her again, but I have a club to protect and a woman to rescue. All for my girl. Hell, I am such a pussy ... but I love the sound of that. *My girl.* Yeah, I could definitely get used to that.

I got out of bed, gathered my clothes and went back to my room. I so wanted to kiss her, but I didn't want to wake her. I also didn't want to answer any questions about where I was going or what I was doing.

I showered and was downstairs making coffee by 6 am. Honey dragged herself into the kitchen, still half asleep. She said, "Ice, you're up early."

"Yeah, got shit to do today. Coffee's still hot. I'll be in my office if anyone is looking for me."

I left the kitchen and headed straight to my office. Today was the day that Skeeter was going to make contact with the Satans. I had to make sure everything was in order. Our plan had to work. We didn't have a lot of time for fuckups. I had been spending too much time thinking about Emma, and we could not afford to have anything go wrong.

I was going through some notes when I heard a knock on the door. What time was it? 10 am already? What the fuck? I'd been holed up in this office for four hours. "Come in."

The door opened and Hawk walked in. "Hey Prez, what's going on? You've been in here for quite some time."

"Just checking and double checking our strategy for tonight. I want us all to get out of this whole, especially Skeeter."

"Ice, he'll be fine. It's not like he is gonna become a Satan. He is just going to give them some intel that will make him their new best friend. Exactly what we need."

"I know you're right, but I can't shake this feeling that something is going to go wrong."

"Ice, you worry too much. The plan is going to go off without a hitch and we are all going to return whole. Now why don't you come out and relax a bit. Your little Emma was asking about you."

I looked up at my VP and best friend. "What'd she say?"

He started to laugh. "I knew it! You're so damn pussy-whipped." He continued to laugh and then added, "I never thought I would see the day when Caden 'Iceman' Jackson was whipped by a chick."

Fuck him. "Are you done?"

His laughter subsided and he turned to leave. "Yeah, I'm done." He chuckled as he left my office.

Asshole. Why do I put up with him? Does the whole club know? They can't. My wing of rooms is on the opposite side of clubhouse, away from everyone else. The only two people in that portion of the building are Emma and me.

Not long after Hawk left, I emerged from my office. I spotted Emma immediately. She was sitting at the bar drinking a cup of coffee. Thank God she wasn't drinking whiskey again. That's a good sign, isn't it? Suddenly, I felt unsure. My confidence wavered and I thought, "*What if she is pissed at me? What if she changed her mind and did not want to be mine? Fuck it, Caden. Stop this right now. Chicks come and go. You can have any pussy you want, even Emma.*"

With a renewed sense of confidence, I walked over to the bar. I leaned down, kissed Emma on the cheek and walked into the kitchen to get myself a cup of coffee. When I returned, all the guys who were sitting around the bar were quietly staring at me.

"What the fuck is wrong with all of you?" I asked.

All at once, the boys suddenly seemed like they had been caught doing something they shouldn't have been. Then there was a mixture of, "Nothing Ice," "No, Prez, we were just hanging out," and, "We're good, Ice." I walked over and seated myself next to Emma, who was giggling to herself. Aw, come on, not her too. Why was
I the laughingstock of the club this morning? Suddenly, the boys sitting at the bar all stepped away from the bar and into the other areas of the common room, giving Emma and I some privacy.

I looked over at Emma and asked, "You too?"

She smiled, "Well, Caden, it seems that the club has never seen you ... well, how did they put it ... claim a woman before." She giggled again.

I leaned in closely to Emma and said, "You sure about this? And keep in mind, you are not just agreeing to be with me. You are agreeing to being with my club. This is my life now."

"Caden, please understand, wanting you has never been a problem. I've always wanted you."

"Why do I feel that the next word out of your mouth is gonna be 'but'?"

"Because it is." I started to speak, but she held up her hand to stop me. "Please hear me out," she asked. I decided to let her speak and nodded reluctantly. "As I said, wanting you has never been a problem. But you live in a world that scares me. The power you have scares me. And it is your life that I am not sure about, not you." She paused for a moment and then added, "But, on the other hand, it is your world that's helping me too. I thought Mark was a stand-up guy, an aspiring attorney ... and now, I am certain that he is the reason that Brianne is gone in the first place." She paused again and I was more confused than ever. Then she said, "I guess what I am trying to say is that what I thought you and your club stood for and what I thought Mark stood for ... well, I was wrong. I judged you both and came to the wrong conclusions. Now, do I think you are a saint? No. But I know you are a good man, Caden, and I trust you with my life."

"So what is it you are trying to say?" I asked hesitantly.

She smiled, "What I am saying, Caden, is that I love you. I've always loved you and yes, I want to be a part of your life. And yes, I understand the club comes with you. If having the club means I get you in the bargain, then it is worth it."

I felt as if my heart was going to explode from my chest. "So you will be my old lady?"

She laughed and said, "Yes, but you are going to have to send me to old lady school."

I laughed. She was amazing, taking all this in for me. I stood and addressed the brothers in the club, "Hey boys … well, it is official. I've finally found a woman who will put up with me and all of you sorry losers." I gestured toward Emma and continued, "My beautiful, sexy, and smart Emma. She has always had my heart and my protection. Now she has my patch."

Everyone cheered and came over to congratulate us. "I don't see a patch. Where's her patch, Prez?" Rebel asked sarcastically.

Well shit, this happened so fast, I didn't think of her "Property of Ice" patch. "Well I guess we'll have to get one made for her, now won't we?" I looked down at Emma and winked.

Emma gave me a curious look, but remained silent. After a few minutes, while the celebration continued, Emma turned to me and asked, "What do you mean when you say that I have your patch?"

She had so much to learn. "Well, darlin', now that you have agreed to be my old lady, you become my property."

"What?" she asked, as if she was mad at me for something.

Brushing her off as I didn't want to create a scene in front of the rest of the club, I said, "We'll talk about this later. Now is not the time."

Now I'd really pissed her off. I could see that vein on the side of her temple pulsating, and I knew that the next words out of her mouth were not going to be pleasant ones. "Now let's get one thing straight, Caden Jackson. I have never been nor will I ever be anyone's property. You got that?"

Everyone in the club fell silent, and all eyes were on Emma and me. Great. I didn't need this, especially not in front of my club. Damn. Knowing that I didn't want to lose my girl, but that I also needed to save face in front of my club, I proceeded with caution. "Emma, let me ask you something." She nodded. Well that was a plus, at least she was keeping her mouth shut. "Are you saying that you do not want to be my old lady?"

Confused, she looked at me and answered, "Of course not. That's not what I am saying at all."

"So you do want to be my old lady?" I asked again.

Meekly, she answered, "Yes."

I grinned and said, "Well then, that's settled."

Again, more confused than before, she asked, "How is this settled?"

"Sweetheart, it comes down to two choices for you. Either you do want to be my old lady or you don't. If you do, then you will wear my property patch. If you don't, then we will settle this mess with Brianne and you will go on your merry way."

She just stood there, staring at me in shock. Then she looked around at everyone around us and suddenly looked embarrassed. She turned back toward me, still silent.

"Well darlin', what's it gonna be?"

Suddenly, she stood a little taller and straightened her shoulders. Not looking embarrassed anymore, she said, "Oh, no! You are not getting rid of me that easy. You're stuck with me!"

Laughing, I pulled her into my arms and said over her shoulder to the club, "Well, I guess *now* it's settled."

CHAPTER 17

Caden

After we all had a celebratory drink in Emma's honor at 10:30 in the morning, I called for a meet with the brothers who would be in on the drive-by tonight. Now that Emma was on board, Honey offered to have Emma's vest and patch made and I agreed. Honey was a champ, and I was proud of her. I knew this had to be hard for her, but she took it all in stride.

Hawk rounded up the rest of the boys that didn't sleep at the clubhouse. By 11:45, all the boys were in the chapel waiting.

We discussed the details of tonight's plan over and over. When everyone had it embedded in their brains what they were to do, the meeting was adjourned. We were all to meet at the clubhouse at 10 pm.

I spent the rest of the day pretty much by myself. I needed a clear head for tonight, so messing around with Emma wouldn't be a good thing, even though I couldn't get her out of my thoughts. Still, Emma had to wait.

At 9:45, the boys started to arrive. We put our cuts on and at approximately 10, we headed out of the compound. We parked our bikes about a block away from Dirty Dick's and waited. Around 10:45, Rebel got the text from Skeeter. It was time. We fired up our bikes and headed toward the bar. As we got closer, we slowed, glancing over to the bar. Just like we planned, twelve Satans were outside, watching. I could only imagine what type of weapons they were brandishing, but then again, they were probably just as well-armed as we were. You can never be too careful in situations like this, and I always make sure my boys are prepared. Once we saw the Satans, we picked up speed and drove off. Phase one of our plan was complete. Now we wait until Skeeter makes contact.

When I got back to the clubhouse, Emma was sitting at the bar talking to Honey. They looked pretty chummy and it appeared that they were becoming friends. Oh damn, I hope they were not comparing notes. Shit. Oh well, I can't change it if they were. I walked over to them and took the seat next to Emma. Honey immediately stepped away and started wiping down the bar. Was it something I said?

Emma looked at me curiously, then asked, "Well?"

I knew what she was asking, but I also needed to make her understand that she couldn't be privy to everything that involved club business. So I played dumb. "Well what?" I asked back.

Frustrated, she asked again, "How did it go tonight?"

Keeping my response as vague as possible, I replied, "It's all good sweetheart. No need to worry your pretty little head about matters that don't concern you."

I'd pissed her off again. She asked, "But Cade?" She wanted to continue to prod me for information, but the look I gave her made it clear that she needed to stop. Thankfully, she got the hint. She was angry, and I knew I would have to deal with that later. She would have to understand. I was not about to explain to her in front of Honey that as a woman, she was not in a position to know about everything we do. I know, it sounds completely sexist, but it is a rule that we abide by on all levels.

I'd planned on having a drink, but decided against it. I was sure that if I lingered at the bar with her, she would find ways to keep prodding and I was not in the mood to deal with it. I got up from the barstool and kissed Emma on the cheek. I started to walk away when Emma called back to me, confusion written all over her face, "Caden?"

"No worries, princess. Just got some work to do."

Sadly, she responded, "Ok."

I went into my office, grabbed my private stash of Maker's and poured myself a drink. My head was pounding and for the first time since Emma has been staying here, I realized this wasn't going to be easy. I thought I could just ease her into club life and there wouldn't be any problems. But, after the whole property conversation this morning and now her wanting details on tonight's run, it's clear that I need to get her straight on a few things. I finished my drink and stepped out of my office. To my surprise, the common area of the clubhouse was dark. The bar was cleaned and everyone was gone. Holy shit, how long was I in my office? I looked at my watch: 3am. Damn ... time flies when your brain is full of shit! I needed to get some sleep.

I headed off to bed. When I got to Emma's room, I was again surprised to find her awake. She was sitting up in bed reading and it appeared as if she was waiting up for me. By the look on her face, I could see she wanted to talk. She wasted no time, either.

"Caden, what's going on?"

"Nothing is going on. Why would you ask a stupid question like that?" I was too tired to give her anything more.

"You were downright rude to me when you came back. I want to know why. I don't appreciate being treated like a dumb blonde! I asked you a question about tonight and you totally blew me off!"

And there it was. I had no choice at this point. She was not going to let me get any sleep unless I talked to her. She wasn't gonna like what I had to say, but she better at least accept it. "Emma, you are *my* old lady. You are no longer considered a civilian in the eyes of this club. Women involved with this club – old ladies, sweetbutts, etc. – they do not get involved with club business. Tonight's run was just that, club business. Not your business. Women are on a need-to-know basis. If I determine that there is something that you need to know, I'll tell you. If I don't, then don't expect me to tell you. The details of tonight's run were not something that I felt you needed to know. Understand?"

"Why are you being so mean?" Tears started to well up in her eyes.

Damnit! Why did she choose to do this at fucking three in the morning? But she was right, I was being harsh. I'm not used to having to answer to the woman in my life. I guess with Emma, things are going to have to be different. We all have a price to pay for the things that we want ... I guess this is mine.

I walked over to the other side of the bed, removed my clothes and crawled into bed next to her. I pulled her toward me and nuzzled her against me. "Emma, I'm sorry. I was rude to you downstairs, but please understand I am not being mean or intentionally being rude. First of all, I've had a long day, and I have a raging headache and a ton of shit on my mind. But that's not an excuse for my behavior." She started to speak, but I took my finger and placed it over her lips. "While I am still awake, let me finish. We have rules. Rules that we all abide by. If the president doesn't follow the rules, then who sets the precedence for the other members of the club to follow them? I should have explained this all to you before, and I didn't. So, I'm gonna explain now. We don't involve our women with club business for their own safety. The less you know, the safer you are. Can you understand that?"

"I do understand, really. But I was so worried for you. I just wanted to know that everyone was alright."

"I know, sweetheart. When it is just you and I, we can have these conversations and I can tell you that everyone is just fine. But in front of the club, the old ladies and sweetbutts, it's just not appropriate. It's my fault; I should have had this talk with you sooner. I just didn't realize how little you knew about club life. I don't mean that in a derogatory way, but in ignorance on my part for not being realistic."

Sheepishly, she asked, "Are you saying you don't think this will work out between you and I?"

I chuckled, "Now young lady, you are putting words in my mouth. No, I am not saying that. I think you are going to make a damn good old lady. What I am saying is that I need to be more understanding of what you don't know." I paused for a moment then added, "Let's do this: how about for now, until I can spend more time with you showing you the ropes around here, if you want to know something or you don't understand something, wait and ask me when we are alone."

"Are you asking me to make you look good in front of your club?" she giggled.

"Yeah, darlin', that's exactly what I am asking you."

"So," she said, as she moved away from me. Getting up from the bed, she stood there staring at me. "How tired are you?" As she said this, she began to lift the tank over her head exposing her bare breasts.

"Well, five minutes ago I was dog tired, but now, I'm thinking not so much."

She grinned and proceeded to remove her panties. She was completely naked and standing at the opposite side of the bed. I couldn't take my eyes off her; her beauty was breathtaking. Why was she just standing there? "Sweetheart, if you don't get your sexy ass over here, I'm comin' to get you."

She got on the bed on her hands and knees and began to crawl over me. When I reached for her, she shooed me away. What the hell? Next thing I knew she had crawled on top of me and was straddling me. I could see the heat in her eyes and it was unlike anything I had ever seen before. She was on fire, and she wanted me.

"So, you've got me here. Now, what are you gonna do with me?" I asked teasingly.

Smugly, she replied, "Look at you."

"I'm right here baby, you can look all you want." Her fingers began to trace the dragon tat that encompassed the upper portion of my chest, his wings and tail trailing down my left arm.

"Your ink is amazing," she said as if she was mesmerized by the color and detail etched into my skin. "Why do you have a dragon?" she asked.

Does she really want to talk at a time like this, or is she just prolonging the inevitable? I could see the passion in her eyes, so I played along. "Well, Ace's road name was Dragon."

"I thought Ace was his road name?" Emma asked.

"Nope, it was Dragon. But more people called him Ace. I really don't know why."

"That's odd, doesn't seem to fit the protocol that I have seen around here."

"No, I guess it doesn't. I never really thought about it, but you are right."

"So, Ace is the reason you got the tattoo?" She urged.

"Yeah, he gave me a life when I had nothing. He was more of a father to me than my own dad was, and I loved him like a father. When he was killed, I had the ink done."

"You don't talk about him much. What was he like?" she asked.

"Emma, do we really have to talk about this now?" I said, exasperated. She must have gotten my message by my tone, because she continued her inspection of my body. Her hands never leave my skin as she studies my ink, tracing the intricate lines. She moves her hand over to my right shoulder and inspects my armor.

"So, this is your armor, because you are a Knight?"

"Yep."

"And the ink on your back?"

"Club name and rocker. All the brothers have one."

"Oh." Her hands moved back to my chest as she ran her fingers lightly over my skin. She leaned over, her nipples hard against my skin and so ready for my attention. I reached up to touch them and again, she shooed my hand away. So, she wants to be in control. I can play ... if that's what she wants.

Her lips press against my neck and trail slowly down my chest until she reaches my nipple. She nipped at it, then grazed me with her teeth. The sensation was amazing and my cock grew harder. She sucked the taut skin into her mouth and I swear I was about to lose control. I'd never had a woman take control over me like this before, and I was finding that I liked it. Her lips moved down my torso until she reached my happy trail. My skin was on fire and I wanted more than anything to be balls deep inside her. She licked along my pelvic bone, purposely avoiding my cock. I couldn't take anymore. "Emma sweetheart, you keep this up and I swear I'm gonna spank your ass."

"Really?" she said excitedly. What. The. Hell. What has happened to my sweet innocent Emma, and where did this fiery sex kitten come from? Holy shit! Just as I was about to reach for her and take matters into my own hands, her mouth descended on my cock. Holy fucking shit. Her luscious mouth was wet, warm, and all over me. It was pure pleasure, and I found myself moving into her mouth. Instead of backing away, she came at me harder, hungrily. Her hand moved up my leg and rested on my balls. She massaged my balls while sucking me from base to tip. There was no turning back, and she continued to work me over. I could feel my cock growing hard, and before I knew it I came harder than I have ever cum before. And to my surprise, she took in every ounce of my juices. Fucking A, that was the best damn blowjob I had ever had.

She crawls up my body and kisses me. I can taste my cum in her mouth, and it is more than erotic. After the kiss, she looks at me and says, "You said that I am your property, right? That I belong to you?"

"Damn straight, sweetheart, you are *my* woman!"

"Well, Caden, my love, now I am telling you, you are mine. My property, my man! There is no turning back now, and I will not share you. Got it?"

"Yes ma'am!" I replied. It was the first time since I was sixteen that I felt totally complete. Now it was my turn.

I reached up and grabbed her head and claimed her mouth, kissing her deep. My hands reached down and grabbed her ass, and I flipped her so that she was on her back. I give her no time to move as my body blanketed her. My cock was hard and throbbing again, and I couldn't wait any longer to be inside her. My cock teased her pussy lips, and finally I was deep inside her. The warmth, the heat, was the most intoxicating feeling I know. I continued to grind into her, her hips meeting my own. Our bodies were slick with sweat as we continued our erotic rhythm. I felt her pussy clench around me and I knew she was close. She called my name as she was about to cum. The combination of our lovemaking and the sound of my name coming from her passion caused me to orgasm with her.

"Holy shit Emma, you are fucking amazing!" I rolled off of her and pulled her in against me.

She snuggled closer to me and said teasingly, "You're not so bad yourself, Prez!"

I laughed and held her close. Quickly my exhaustion caught up with me and I was asleep.

CHAPTER 18

Caden

We still hadn't heard from Skeeter. I was beginning to worry, and the boys were getting antsy. Finally, five days after the drive-by, I received a text from Skeeter: "Meet me at Betty's, 30 minutes." I rounded up Rebel and Ryder and we headed to Betty's Dinor. When we got there, Skeeter was already there, waiting.

We headed over to his table and sat down. "Whatcha got?"

"Ice, it was awesome. At first I was scared, I didn't know any of them. But I got in the bar and I found a guy named Skid – he had a VP patch. I walked up to him and told him that I had overheard some guys in leather vests outside talking about raiding the bar. They bought it, hook, line, and sinker. Skid went over to another guy, Gypsy – he's their president, you know – and they rounded up about ten more guys and headed outside. That's when I texted Rebel."

"So what happened after the setup?"

Skeeter continued, "Well, I thought it would be too obvious if I went outside with them, so I stayed put, pulled up a seat at the bar and ordered a drink. About fifteen minutes later, they all came back in. Skid and Gypsy walked over to me and sat down on the bar stools on either side of me." He paused for a few seconds and continued. "They thanked me for the intel and then we just hung out. They asked a lot of personal questions. I gave them as many honest answers as I could without giving my cover away, or my

126

association with the Knights. I figured that if they checked me out, it needed to be accurate or we would be back to square one." Smart guy. I knew we picked the right guy to do this job.

I was getting frustrated. I knew he needed to tell us everything, but I wanted him to get to the info he'd found out. But, I tried to remain patient and listen.

Rebel, however was not as patient as me. He asked, "So why did it take you five days to make contact?"

Skeeter looked as if he had been waiting for us to ask that. What the hell? "Well, that's the good part. Before the night was over they invited me back to their clubhouse for a party. Those boys can party, let me tell you. Before I left their clubhouse, I was invited to another party on Saturday. So I went. I ended up spending Saturday night in one of their rooms. I haven't been back since, but I figured it would be best to lay low for a few days instead of running immediately to you."

I was a little suspicious as to why Skeeter couldn't have at least called us, but I decided not to mention anything now. If he were hiding anything from us, the truth would come out eventually. It always does. For now, my priority was to find out what he knew. We still may need him down the road. Besides, he did do a good job and got himself in with the Satans. Perhaps he thought that any contact could jeopardize the relationship that he'd started with them. "So, did you find out anything we can use? Did you see Grayson? Brianne?"

"I'm getting there, be patient. Yeah, Grayson was at the clubhouse Friday night, but I didn't speak to him. He was drinking heavily and complaining about some chick. I think her name was Emma. I did hear him say to Gypsy that he wanted him to 'get her', but I didn't get all the details."

That fucking son of a bitch! He's put a mark on my girl! "What else?" My patience was wearing thin.

"So, that was all I got on Friday, but Saturday was a different story. I got to the clubhouse around 9:30 and the party was already hopping. Skid came down the stairs with a woman. From the picture you gave me, I think it was Brianne ... but she was so drugged out, it was hard to tell. She had a black eye and her left cheek was all swollen. She could barely stand, unless she was leaning on Skid. Grayson showed up around 11. Again, he started drinking. Lucky for me, he sat right next to me at the bar. He kept referring to this Emma chick and calling her a fucking bitch. He was pissed about something, and he kept saying that if things went his way, he wouldn't have all these problems. Gypsy came over and sat next to him. Grayson had had so much to drink that discretion was not on the top of his list. He asked Gypsy how Skid was doing working Brianne over. Gypsy responded that it was going good and that she wouldn't talk anymore, that she had learned her place. Grayson was pleased, but then said something to the effect that Emma had left him and that what they did to Brianne didn't matter anymore. He told Gypsy that they could let her go. Gypsy said at this point Brianne knew too much about the club and that they were not going to let her go. Now, Grayson was more interested in getting revenge on Emma and again asked Gypsy to bring her in – whatever that meant. Gypsy refused. Then Grayson mentioned you. He was rambling; he said that you took everything from him including Emma. He said that you and Emma go way back. Said she fucking talked about you all the time. He wanted Gypsy to kill you and take down the Knights. Gypsy refused again. Said that although there was an ongoing feud between the clubs, and their plan was to eventually take over the Knights' territories, they were not ready for an all-out war. And, taking down a club president would cause just that. Grayson got angry and started yelling at Gypsy, saying 'you son of a bitch, you owe me. I've saved your ass on numerous occasions.' Gypsy remained calm and motioned to one of the other members, a big guy; I didn't know his name. He came over, and Gypsy told him to dispose of the trash. Grayson got angry and left on his own."

My senses were now on high alert. I swear that I could actually feel the blood running through my veins. I had the feeling that he was holding something back, so I had to ask, "Anything else?"

Skeeter hesitated and looked at me worried. *What the fuck?* "Skeeter, spit it out. I know there is more. I need to know everything."

He nodded, then paused for a moment. "You're right, there is one more thing."

"What?"

"I have reason to believe that Grayson is going to take matters into his own hands. After Gypsy refused him, like I said, Grayson was pissed. As he got up from the barstool, he mumbled under his breath something to the effect that if the Satans weren't gonna help him, he would take down you and your whole fucking club by himself. I heard that part clear as day."

Holy fucking shit. I was right, there is more to this – and I'd done the right thing in keeping Emma here. But now, with this info, we are all in danger. I need to get Emma out of town. If Grayson plans to attack my club, Emma can't be at the clubhouse. My boys can handle a situation like this, but Emma can't. I don't know what this asshole has against my club, but I have to make sure everyone stays safe. We need to get back to the clubhouse. "Skeeter, you did great. Thanks for the intel. We've got to get back. Keep the friendship with the Satans going."

Confused, Skeeter asked, "You still want me to hang with them?"

"Yeah, I do. We need to keep someone on the inside for now. You cool with that?"

"Sure Ice, whatever you need," Skeeter agreed.

As we started to head out of the diner, I turned back to Skeeter, "Just don't wait days to make contact. The more intel we get, the better. You got me?"

Skeeter nodded. "Sure do, Ice. You can count on me."

CHAPTER 19

Emma

Over the last week, I've spent most of my time with Honey, and we are actually becoming friends. Cade has been so busy and standoffish. I know he is worried, but for what, I have no idea. It had been several days since Friday night, the night that Cade explained to me that old ladies are not privy to club business and if there was something I needed to know, he would tell me. His message was clear: Don't ask. But I know his worrying has something to do with Brianne and Mark.

Honey and I were talking over coffee when we heard a lot of commotion in the common area of the clubhouse: doors banging and lots of yelling. When we stepped into the doorway from the kitchen, we could see that Cade, Rebel, and Ryder had returned, and not one of them was looking very happy. They walked in and headed straight for Cade's office. He was barking orders as he came through the clubhouse, and the last thing I heard was, "Church! Now!" I looked over at Honey, who looked worried. Something bad must have happened.

"What do you think is going on?" I asked.

Honey shook her head and said, "My guess is that their meeting with Skeeter didn't go very well. Ice does not hide his emotions very well when he is pissed off." She knows him so well. And how did she know they were meeting with Skeeter? I thought women were on a need-to-know basis? I still found that I got jealous of her; she knew him so much better than I did. She knew how to be his old lady and exactly what he expects of her. He is just so different than when we were kids, but on rare occasions, when we were alone, I saw the boy I knew coming out.

"What do you think happened?" I was beginning to worry. Maybe they found out something about Brianne?

Honey turned to go back in the kitchen and I followed. She stopped by the sink and said, "Hell if I know, Emma. These boys try to do good, but they always seem to get themselves caught up in some shit. It could be anything."

"Maybe we should go find out?" I asked.

"No!" Honey yelled. "Women aren't allowed. We do not participate in their meetings and we definitely are not privy to what they do, even old ladies. The quicker you learn and accept that, the easier things will be for you."

Well, crap. That was the same speech I got from Cade the other night. I had never been one to just sit idly by and wait to be told anything. It was driving me crazy. But, I knew if I wanted this life with Cade, I needed to abide by the club rules. Perhaps when I get Cade alone, he may choose to tell me what's happened. He did say that I could ask him stuff in private. Damn, the waiting sucks!

Honey and I finished up in the kitchen and headed out into the common area. She was cleaning up the bar from last night and I offered to help. I was just so bored with sitting around. Yeah, sure, I was able to get some work done, but staying here day in and day out was getting on my nerves. Just as we finished getting the bar cleaned up, the guys emerged from their meeting. They all headed to the bar. When Honey saw them, she proceeded to get several shots and a couple of beers. Hell, she even knew what these guys drank. When the boys got to the bar, they downed their drinks.

Cade leaned over the bar, kissed my cheek, and whispered in my ear, "We need to talk."

"Ok," I replied sheepishly. I was nervous. Something bad must have happened, I just knew it. I wondered how much he would tell me. I came out from behind the bar. Caden turned and walked toward his office and I followed. I felt like I was heading to the principal's office.

When we got to his office, he closed the door behind me and said, "Sit down." I sat down. What else could I do?

I remained quiet while he paced the room. Then he began to speak. "Emma, we've heard some information today that I don't think you are going to like."

"Caden, I'm a grown woman. Just tell me."

He continued, "We've found Brianne. She is being held in the Satans' clubhouse."

"Is she ok?"

"We don't know. Has she ever done drugs?"

What the hell? I don't ever remember Brianne doing drugs. "No! Absolutely not."

"That's what I figured. It appears that the Satans are drugging her to keep her quiet about something. From what we can figure out, they are using the drugs to keep her just enough out of it to not care about keeping in touch with family or friends."

"Oh my God, this can't be true!" I said, devastated. "Why are they doing this to her?"

Caden sighed and hesitated for a moment. "Well, it seems to lead back to you and Grayson. We know for sure that Grayson initiated the Satans' involvement with Brianne. Based on what you told me about Grayson, my guess is that he wanted to keep her from telling you the truth about him."

"Oh Caden, I was so wrong about him." I felt like crawling into a hole. This was happening to Brianne because of me. "So what do we do now?"

He shrugged and turned away from me. Something else was wrong. He took a few steps and then turned back toward me. "Emma, there's more." Afraid of what he was going to say next, I waited in silence. "From what we have been told, she has been badly beaten. She has a black eye and a swollen cheek. I don't know who did it, but from the intel that we have received, I am guessing it was Skid. We all know that the Satans in general treat their women like shit, but they are saints compared to Skid. He is the worst of them all."

I was horrified. I began to cry uncontrollably. How could things get this bad? Caden came over to me and pulled me into his arms. He held me for the longest time. I just couldn't believe this was happening. Then, after several minutes, I said, "Caden, you have to get her out of there. Please." I pleaded, "Promise me you will get her out."

"I'll do everything in my power to get her out, I promise. But, Emma, there is more."

What now? I don't think I can take any more.

"Grayson has asked the Satans to take you in."

Sniffling, I asked, "What does that mean?"

"Basically, he wants them to take you like they did Brianne. I don't know what his plans are, but you are not safe. I thought by keeping you at the clubhouse, I could keep you safe. But, with the information that I learned today, I realize I was being foolish and I can't. I need to get you away from here and out of Edinboro. Grayson knows you are with us, and he has not only targeted you, but my club as well. I'm taking you away. We have several safe houses across the country. We are leaving first thing in the morning."

"But Cade, I can't ...."

He interrupted me and said, "Do not question me on this! It is not open for discussion. Be sure to have you bags packed first thing in the morning." He moved to the door and opened it, which I interpreted as my cue to leave.

CHAPTER 20

Caden

I hated being so harsh with Emma, but she needed to understand the severity of this. She also needed to understand that I would do everything in my power to keep her safe. I've waited too long to get her back in my life, I won't lose her now.

After Emma left, I called Hawk. I didn't know if he was still at the clubhouse and it was just easier to call his cell. It turns out he was already heading to my office – as he answered his phone, he also opened my office door. "Hey Ice, what's up?" he said as he entered my office.

I clicked off my phone and said, "I'm sure you know that I have spoken with Emma. I'm getting her out of here first thing in the morning."

"Are you going, too?"

"That was my plan. Why?" Of course I was going, why would he ask me that?

"Well, Ice, just hear me out, ok?"

"What?" I was getting frustrated. What was he thinking?

"I think it would be best if you had Rebel take her. They will be expecting you to be with her, so they will be watching you – especially now that they know the two of you are connected. If Rebel takes her, he can make sure she is safe. He can get her settled and then when we get this shit settled, you can go to her or bring her home. Just think about it. I'm just looking out for you and your girl."

If I thought logically, he was right. But, if I had to be honest with myself, I didn't think logically where Emma was concerned. I thought about what he said for a few minutes and finally I agreed. He was right. "Fine, get Reb in here." Hawk left my office and in a couple of minutes, he returned with Rebel.

"What's up, boss?" he asked as he came into my office.

"I want you to plan on taking Emma to our safe house in Rome."

"When?"

"First thing in the morning. Her safety is your top priority. Got it?"

"Got it. I'll protect her with my life. You gonna be ok here without me?"

I knew why he asked that. As my sergeant at arms, it was his job to have my back. He was my protection. But right now, Emma mattered more. I could take care of myself if I needed to. I mean really, I had 24 other brothers with me. "Yeah, I'll be fine – especially if I know that Emma is safe. Her safety is my priority. We got enough guys here to take care of the club. Plan on staying with her for a while, until we get a handle on things here. I should be up within the week."

"Ok Prez. Consider it done. Anything else?"

"Nope, we're good here. Thanks." I knew he realized how important Emma's safety was to me and I knew she would be in good hands, but I still couldn't help worrying. Our safe house in Rome was the perfect location to keep her safe. It was nestled in upstate New York, surrounded by lots of trees, and bordered up to Delta Lake State Park. Quiet and serene, just what Emma needed.

"Hawk, wait a minute."

"Yeah?"

"Thanks. That was a good call."

"Sure thing, it's what I do." He turned to leave.

"Wait, one more thing. Make sure Rebel takes Emma's phone. Give him a couple of burners. If Grayson has her cell number, I don't want him to track her. Nor do I want him calling her, either."

"You got it," he said and left my office.

Now that my first order of business was handled, it was time to move on to the next. How in the fuck are we gonna get Brianne out? The guys had some ideas today at the meet, but nothing seemed to be right. There had to be a way, but how?

I sat down at my desk and contemplated all that had happened over the last week and a half. Then I realized, I needed to have Skeeter find out where in their clubhouse they were keeping Brianne. That would be a start. So, I sent him a text with further instructions.

Several hours had passed and I realized that I had been in my office longer than I had intended. I needed my girl. I headed out to the common room, but she was nowhere to be found. I asked Honey and she said that Emma had some packing to do and had gone upstairs. Perfect, exactly where I wanted her.

I headed upstairs and turned toward Emma's room. Her door was slightly ajar, so I took it as an invitation, hoping she was waiting for me. As I walked in I could see that she was diligently packing, just as I'd instructed. Good girl. She didn't notice me, or she was pretending not to notice me. "Emma?" I said softly. She slowly looked up at me, her eyes fixated on mine. Neither of us spoke, and I found it very difficult to look away from her beautiful body in her little boy shorts and tank top. Damn, she was so sexy. I knew that one of us needed to say something, but I was finding that all I could think about was that I needed her. Since I came here for a reason, that someone needed to be me. I couldn't be anything more than honest with her. "I need you." One simple statement that said everything she needed to hear. She didn't need any further invitation than what I offered, and she came to me eagerly. I placed my hand behind her neck, threading my fingers into her hair, and pulled her toward me with urgency, pressing her body against my own. I couldn't wait any longer, and I devoured her lips with so much need and intensity it was as if her mouth was my only form of survival. I pulled at her tank top as she lifted her hands over her head, breaking our kiss briefly to remove it. "Tell me you want this."

Breathlessly she replied, "Yes, I want this."

My lips crashed down on hers again. The urgency built throughout my entire body and I realized I couldn't wait any more. I pulled away from our kiss and I took her head in my hands. As I gazed into her eyes, I told her exactly what I needed. "I need to be inside you, Emma, now. After the day I have had, you are like coming home: my solace, my comfort. Now that I have had a taste of you, I can't get enough."

She inched closer, inviting me. "Caden, you are all that to me, too. You make me feel safe and protected. It's always been you and it always will be." That was all I needed to hear. I guided her to the door. I raised both her hands over her head and pinned them in place with one hand. My other hand stroked her breast. As her nipple beaded to a peak, she began to moan, causing me to become more eager.

I reached for the waistband of her shorts and slid them down just enough so that they rested on her pelvic bone. I glanced down her body and could see the peak of her mound and my mouth began to water. "God baby, you are so damn beautiful. You smell so sexy, are you ready for me?" She nodded. Oh no, a simple nod was not going to work for me. I needed to hear the words. I stepped back slightly. "Tell me," I demanded.

She looked up to me submissively and softly said with a stutter, "Y-Yes." I dropped to my knees, kneeling before her and I took in her intoxicating scent. I was at her mercy as I slowly began to worship her. I slid her shorts down all the way to the floor and she quickly stepped out of them. With her incredible sweetness displayed for only me to see, I couldn't stay away any longer. I leaned down and kissed her thigh, trailing kisses up her to her core. My tongue probed at her clit and I began to lick, running my tongue up and around her. I glanced up at her and I saw that she was watching my every move. My erection began to burn and strain against my jeans. She was still watching me as she began to run her fingers through my hair, pulling me toward her pelvis. I had never seen so much desire in her eyes. She started to moan again and her hips began to move with the same rhythm as my tongue. I continued to lick as her orgasm raged inside her, allowing her to ride it out. Slowly, I stood up and moved to kiss her luscious lips, making her taste herself on me. She didn't even hesitate. She was on fire, and I couldn't wait any longer to be inside her. I quickly unbuttoned and unzipped my jeans, lowering them just enough to free my straining cock. She looked down at me and before I knew it, she had dropped to her knees. Holy fuck!

She wrapped her mouth around the head of my cock and began to suck, hard, hungrily. She stopped briefly and licked me from balls to tip, once, then twice. "God damnit Emma, you are so damn good with your mouth. I don't know how much more I can take," I groaned. She continued sucking and licking and I felt my body tense. I was about to cum, but I realized that I didn't want it that way. I needed to be inside her. I gently pulled her up to me, making her stop, and she gave me a look of disappointment. "No worries, darlin'. I just need to be inside you."

I carefully guided her back over to the bed. Before she knew any different my body had blanketed hers, rubbing myself on her thigh with my cock. She pleaded, "Caden, please. Don't make me wait any longer." Her need was intoxicating.

Fuck, I just realized I didn't have a condom. "Emma, sweetheart, are you on the pill?" She nodded. That was all I needed to hear. With that, I began to thrust into her. I could feel every part of her as her pussy walls began to clench onto me. I slowly started to build momentum, then began picking up the pace. I couldn't stop my hands from roaming all over her beautiful body.

Her hands grabbed onto my back as she dug her nails in, pulling at me to get closer. We were so close, our bodies molded together. I took my hand and slid it between us, then began to rub my thumb softly over her clit. She cried out, "Harder! Caden, harder! I need more." I slammed into her, hard, putting myself balls deep into her. Her body began to tense, her walls tightened their hold on me, and finally she let go. "Caden!" I continued to thrust into her as her pussy continued to clench and milk my dick. It was my undoing, and I came harder than I ever had before. We rode out our orgasms together, and after, we lay together for a long time. I was still inside her, and the last thing I wanted to do was to leave her warmth and softness. But I knew I needed to and I slowly slid out of her, watching my dick come out of her pussy glistening with our combined juices. I watched as what I'd left behind slowly dripped down her thighs; it was the sexiest thing I had ever seen.

Finally, I got up and walked toward the bathroom. Sleepily, she asked, "Where are you going?" I didn't respond, but emerged from the bathroom with a warm washcloth. I gently cleaned her and she purred like a kitten. When I was done, I climbed back into bed, pulled her toward me, and fell into a deep, sated sleep.

CHAPTER 21

Emma

I woke up early, sweating. It wasn't hard to figure out why – I soon realized that I was entangled in Caden's grasp. Ever so quietly I managed to wiggle out of his hold. He didn't wake, but rolled over with a moan. I stood there and stared at him for a while. He was absolutely beautiful, and I had to pinch myself to convince myself that this all wasn't a dream. I had dreamt about being with Cade for so long, and finally I was here. I was his old lady.

I went in to shower and when I emerged, Caden was awake. I said, "Good morning, sleepyhead. Sleep well?"

He smiled groggily and said, "Hell yeah." He paused for a moment; taking in my wet body covered only in a towel, and then said, "Come here, beautiful." How could a girl resist that? I sauntered over to him and sat down next to him on the bed. He rose up and kissed me on the cheek, rubbing his thumb across my collarbone.

"What time are we leaving?" I asked. Suddenly, he got a worried look on his face. "Caden, what's wrong?"

He didn't respond right away, and I was beginning to worry. He rubbed his face with his hands, pushed one back through his hair, and then said, "Emma, I'm not going with you."

"What?" I couldn't believe what I was hearing. He was going to send me off by myself! "What do you mean you are not going with me? Caden, this was your idea, not mine. This isn't a vacation; we were going away to be safe. Your words, not mine!" I was angry. How dare he do this to me?

"I know, and you are still going away. But you are going with Rebel."

"But why? Don't you want to be with me?" I knew that was such a girly thing to say, but I just couldn't help it. After last night, I just didn't understand.

"I can't believe you just asked me that. Are you fucking serious? I don't even think I should grace that question with an answer. You fucking know better!" he yelled.

"Caden, I'm sorry. But what do you expect me to think?"

"Well if you would let me finish and stop jumping to conclusions, perhaps you will understand *why* I am not going with you."

Feeling ashamed now, I replied, "Ok."

He then continued, "I'm not going with you because you will be safer without me. Grayson and the Satans have tied you to me. They know we share a past. They will have their eyes on me. If I go with you, I'll be leading them right to us. Rebel is my sergeant at arms. I know you are not familiar with what that title means, but putting it simply, he's my enforcer. Plus, he excels at staying under the radar. I trust the man with my life, and yours. So, he is taking you to New York. He will stay with you until we settle this ordeal with the Satans. I don't know how long this is going to take, but I'll be able to think more clearly knowing that you are far away from here." He paused for a moment and then added, "Now do you understand?"

"I do, but ... I don't know him." How could I spend a few days in a house with a man I don't know? Suddenly I was more scared than I had been before.

"Well, sweetheart, I suggest you get to know him – strictly platonically, I might add."

What could I do? Refuse to go? That would never work. Caden would bind and gag me to make sure I left with Rebel. I had no choice but to agree.

Caden reached over to the nightstand and looked at his phone. "Fuck, it's 6. We gotta move." He jumped out of bed and headed toward the bathroom. I watched as his naked body casually walked about my room as if he didn't have a care in the world. When he got to the bathroom, he poked his head out and said, "Put your bags by the door. I'll carry them down when I am done. Be done in 10." He disappeared into the bathroom. A few minutes later, I heard the shower.

I sat down on the bed, totally drained. The past week and a half had been a total whirlwind. My best friend disappeared, I'd been uprooted from my home, I'd called off my engagement, my life was in danger, and now, I was heading to New York with a man I didn't know. But Cade said that he trusts him. I trust Cade. I trust Cade with my life. So, if this was what he thought is best, I could do it. I had to. The last thing I wanted to do was to add more to Caden's plate. I've already done enough.

Caden emerged from the shower looking delicious. Oh hell, I wish we had more time – or that I just wasn't leaving. But it would have to wait. He left my room with a towel wrapped around his waist, his hair dripping wet. When he returned, he was dressed in jeans and a black t-shirt, and his hair was brushed back. It occurred to me that sometimes, it is more arousing looking at a man fully clothed, in the right clothes, than seeing him naked.

"Ready to go, darlin'? he asked as he was grabbing my bags.

"Yep, lead the way," I said as I followed him out the door.

When we got downstairs, Rebel was sitting at the bar drinking coffee. God, that sounded so good. "Caden, do we have some time for me to get some coffee?"

"Sure, but make it quick," he replied. I ran into the kitchen and poured myself a cup of the most wonderful thing God had ever created. To my surprise, I found creamer in the fridge. That's funny ... they never had cream before. I always had to use milk. Hmmmm. Honey must have gotten it. Perhaps I was starting to grow on her.

I came back out to the bar and saw Cade and Rebel talking in hushed tones. My guess is that it was club business. I remembered what Cade and Honey told me about old ladies being on a need-to-know basis. So, I plopped myself down in a barstool at the other end of the bar so they didn't think I was eavesdropping.

A few minutes later, Cade walked over and kissed my forehead. I loved it when he did that. It reminded me so much of when we were kids. He always took care of me then, and he is taking care of me now. "It's time for you two to head out. You good?"

I replied reassuringly, "I am." I hesitated for a moment and then said, "Everything is going to be ok. I just know it." He smiled. He grabbed my bags and headed out the door and I followed. Rebel came up behind us and unlocked the steel gray Durango that was parked by the door. Thank God we were not going on a bike. I had been wondering about that and how that would work. It's a good thing I don't have to find out.

My bags were loaded and we were ready to go. Rebel got in the vehicle and I hesitated for a moment. I looked up at Caden, not wanting to say goodbye. I didn't know when I was going to see him again and I didn't want to leave him. I kept telling myself that I was going to see him in a few days, but it wasn't helping. Caden pulled me into his arms and held me close. He bent down and kissed me. Not a little peck, but a real kiss. I melted against him, wanting more, but knowing I was not going to get anything more. I had to leave. He released me and I stepped toward the car, but then I hesitated and turned back. I hugged Caden once more and whispered in his ear, "I love you." Not waiting for a response, I turned and got in the car. I didn't need a response; I knew how he felt.

Rebel pulled out and the tears started to fall. I couldn't help it; the last thing I wanted was to leave Caden. Not now, not ever! "Emma, everything is going to be ok. That's what I heard you say to Ice, and I know you believe it," Rebel said, trying to make me feel better.

"I do believe it. It's just so hard."

"I know, been in the same type of situation myself. It's not fun leaving the ones you love, but sometimes it is the best thing for them." He said this rather sadly, and I made a mental note to ask him about it later. He then added, "Oh, before I forget, give me your phone."

"What?"

"Emma, you need to give me your phone."

"Why?"

"Because I need to destroy it."

Suddenly, I was not sad anymore, I was mad. "You are not taking my phone!" I yelled.

"Emma, you don't understand." He pulled another phone out of his pocket and handed it to me. "This is a burner. It is a cell phone with service, but it is untraceable. Your phone is traceable. You keep your phone, you use it, and our hideout is no longer secret. Now, give me your phone."

"Oh ok ... but all my contacts?"

"Back it up, then hand it over. For the next several days, the only number you will need is Ice's."

I quickly opened up my backup app and got it running. About 5 minutes later, my contacts were backed up. I removed my phone case. It was Kate Spade – I wasn't gonna have him destroy that. I handed my phone to Rebel, and he chucked it out the window. That was the latest iPhone, with all the bells and whistles, including Siri! Damn, now I am stuck with this stupid flip phone. At least I had all my contacts backed up, so when I do get a new phone, I won't lose anything. Thank goodness for the Cloud!

CHAPTER 22

Caden

Emma and Rebel had only been gone 10 minutes and already I wanted to get on my bike and go after them. I just needed to keep myself busy until Rebel checked in. It was still early, so I decided to head over to Betty's for some breakfast.

When I got back to the clubhouse, I headed straight to my office. I still hadn't heard from Rebel and I was getting antsy. I started doing some research of my own on Mark Grayson. I figured the more informed I was, the better off we would be for taking him down and getting Brianne. What I found didn't surprise me. Gypsy, the president of the Satans MC, had faced a murder rap about a year ago. It was basically an open-and-shut case, but the case was thrown out due to some new evidence that they found. What did surprise me was that Grayson had represented the bastard. Now that I see the connection, my guess is that that's probably where their relationship started. The article I found didn't disclose the exact nature of the new evidence, so I decided to keep digging.

About an hour after I had immersed myself in the world of Mark Grayson, I hit the jackpot. Apparently the new evidence was a young female eyewitness in her early twenties, who had claimed that Gypsy was not the murderer. She testified in a deposition that the killer was blond, in his thirties, and of a large build. It was the exact opposite of Gypsy's description – he was small, had dark brown hair, and was about fifty years old. So they threw the case out. Interesting. The girl looked so damn familiar too, but I couldn't place where I had seen her before. I needed to find out some more about this girl. I called Dbag on his cell.

He answered on the first ring. "Hey Ice. What's up?"

"I need you to check something out for me. Look into a girl named Peyton Anderson. She is probably in her early- to mid-twenties, and about a year ago she lived in Waterford. I'm sending over a pic and an article I found online about her. See what you can find."

"You got it, Prez. I'm on it." Man, he loved this shit. He totally missed his calling. He should be working for the CIA or the FBI. But I'm glad he's not and belongs to us. There are days I would be lost without his expertise.

As soon as I got off the phone, I got a text from Rebel.

> Been driving for two hours. Emma is hungry. Stopping in Buffalo for breakfast and gonna pick up some groceries for the safe house. All is good. Will text you when we get to Rome.

Thank fuck ... so far they are safe. Then it occurred to me, I forgot to remind him about her phone – and I just remembered she took her laptop. Shit. I immediately texted Rebel back.

> Forgot to remind you to get Emma's phone. Hoping that you took care of that. Also, take that laptop away from her. I don't want her on the Internet or doing anything that can divulge your location.

He texted back.

> Phone is destroyed. She has the burner. I'll get the laptop. No worries. She's in good hands.

> I know, brother, thanks!

I knew she was in good hands. I totally trusted Rebel, but not being able to look after her myself was making me crazy. This shit better get straightened out fast so I can get my girl back.

Forty-five minutes later, my phone rang. I glanced down and saw that it was Dbag. Damn he was fast. I answered the call, "Whatcha got?"

"Ice, this shit is fucked up." I could hear the excitement in his voice and I knew he'd found something good. He continued, "This Peyton chick – she was engaged to Grayson five years ago. I found their engagement announcement, along with a public notice that the wedding was postponed indefinitely and a location where folks could pick up the gifts they sent, if they wanted them back. It was cancelled one week before the wedding."

"What the hell? What else?"

"I could trace her for about six months after the scheduled wedding; she did a lot of traveling. Then, nothing. Peyton basically disappeared after that. I mean *really* disappeared. Nothing. No financial transactions, no job, nothing. It was like she never existed. Then, wham, she shows up as a surprise witness in the Gypsy case last year."

"Shit! Can you find anything on her now?"

"Yeah, she moved back to Waterford. Lives in a small house by herself." He hesitated for a moment and then added, "Are you sitting down?"

Fuck, this didn't sound good. "Yeah, I'm sitting. Spill it."

"She's one of ours."

"What?"

"She works at Kandi's. She's one of the strippers."

So that's why she looked familiar to me. Kandi's Gentlemen's Club was one of our clubs. We employed a lot of girls, and I couldn't possibly remember all their names. "Damn! This is not good, Dbag. Not good at all. I need you to round up Ryder and Hawk for me and get your asses here. We need to make a visit to Ms. Anderson today."

"You got it! We'll be there in thirty." He hung up the phone. I got on my computer and began to scroll through the employee files of Kandi's. Fucking A, she was right there under our nose all the time. Was she a mole? Had the Satans planted her here? Or could this be coincidence? Hell if I knew, but I was about to find out.

I heard the rumble of bikes and knew it was my boys. I grabbed my keys and headed out. They were getting ready to dismount their bikes when I came out. "Get back on your bikes, boys, we're leaving now." I fired up my Harley and we peeled out.

It was late morning and there were only a few cars in Kandi's parking lot. We parked our bikes and went in. Callie Rae, the manager, was tending bar for a few regulars who had come in for their morning drinks. She didn't notice us when we walked in, but by the time we got to the bar, Callie asked, "What brings you boys here today?"

I spoke up, "Morning, Callie. You got someone here to watch the bar? We need to talk to you." She got a worried look on her face, nodded, and then picked up the house phone. I couldn't hear what she said, but a few seconds later, one of the girls came up. She smiled at us and stepped behind the bar. Callie came out and we followed her to her office.

When we got to the office, she turned to me and said, "What's going on?"

I tried to reassure her that nothing was wrong, "Nothing is wrong, if that's what you are thinking." She breathed a sigh of relief. "I'm looking for Peyton Anderson."

"Has she done something? I have these girls drug tested regularly, Ice." She was on the defensive, and I guess I really couldn't blame her. She'd taken good care of these girls and had never given us a reason to question anything she did. She was a valued employee.

"Nope, it's not like that. We just need to talk to her. Is she here?"

She calmed down a bit and looked behind her to the schedule on the wall. "She comes in at two."

"Ok. You are going to need to find a replacement for her. She won't be working today." I looked over to Ryder and said, "Ryder, stick around. When she gets here, bring her to the clubhouse. It's better that we talk to her there."

"Will do," he replied. Hawk, Dbag, and I left. We went straight back to the clubhouse to wait for Ryder to get back with Peyton.

CHAPTER 23

Emma

Rebel and I had been driving for a few hours now. We stopped for breakfast and to buy some things to stock the kitchen at the safe house. We had about an hour to go and I was going stir-crazy. Rebel didn't talk much, so I decided to engage him in some conversation.

"Rebel? Can I ask you something?"

"Sure, but I may not answer." Now that was a typical guy response. But really, had I expected any different?

"Is Rebel your real name, or is it a road name?"

He glanced over to me, surprised by my question. "Yes, it is a road name." No elaboration, just that short answer.

"What is your real name?"

"Balefire."

"Is that your first name?"

"Yes, O'Byrne is my last name."

"You're Irish!"

He smiled and said, "Yes, I am."

"So am I!" I was so excited that we had something in common. It wasn't much, but it was a start. If I was going to spend the next few days with this man, I would take anything. "My last name is Baylee!"

He glanced over to me with an odd look on his face and said sarcastically, "That's great. Makes us kindred spirits or something like that."

Figures. Guys just don't get it. We women need to have conversation. Men can sit in silence forever and brood, but women need to talk. I swear as soon as they figure that out, there will be no mystery between the sexes.

Just then my phone beeped. I glanced down, not familiar with the sounds that this phone made, and saw that it was a text from Caden.

> I miss you. Don't forget, you are safe. You are my family now, which means you are part of the club. The club will do everything in its power to keep you safe.

That was odd. I knew he was trying to reassure me, but this whole club life was still new to me. I just didn't understand the whole family thing. Then I decided, perhaps I could use this time with Rebel to get a little education on *"the club."* I quickly texted a response back to Caden.

> I miss you too! Thank you! I love you!

I waited a minute or two and got no return response. Ok. I could wait. I knew he loved me. I knew he would tell me one day. I just needed to be patient. I put my phone back in my purse. Rebel asked, "Was that Ice?"

"Yes." I didn't elaborate.

"Something up?" he asked.

Well, perhaps I should keep him informed. After all, my life is in his hands for the next few days. "He just wanted to let me know that I was safe now; that the club was my family now." I didn't think I needed to tell him about the "missing you" part. That was private, between Caden and me.

"He's right about that. You are family. You are Ice's old lady now. His queen. You are just as much a part of this club as I am, or Hawk, or any of the brothers."

I still did not get all this, but this was the perfect opportunity to ask. "Rebel, why are you part of the club? I mean, how did you get involved with them?"

He glanced over to me and I got the feeling that he didn't want to talk about it, but he surprised me and said, "When I met Ace, there was shit going on in my life; things that I would rather not talk about. But let's just say Ace and this club saved my life in more ways than one."

Confused, I asked, "The same Ace that Caden told me about?"

He got a sad look on his face, and then said, "Yeah, the same one. Ace was VP when I joined the club. He is the one who sponsored Ice and nominated him for SAA, then when the Satans killed Red – our president – Ace nominated Ice for VP. When Ace died in a war with the Satans, Ice was voted in as president and took over the club. I believe that Ice looked to Ace as a father figure, especially after losing his own." Caden had already told me all of that, but I didn't want to lose the conversation I had going so I just nodded and listened. It's comforting to know that Cade had someone to turn to and look up to after his parents died. It always made me sad that Caden had never gotten along with his dad, they were so different in so many ways. I remember him always complaining about his dad not understanding or his dad making him make life choices that he had no interest in.

"I see. Was Ice already a member of the club when you joined, or did he join after you?" I asked. I figured the more information I could get out of Rebel, the better for me.

"Yes, he was." Again, he didn't elaborate.

"So, do you consider the club your family like Caden – I mean, Ice – does?" I needed to know if it was just Cade who felt that way, or if all of them did.

"Absolutely. I would have no family without the club. You see, Emma, what you don't understand is that the Knights are just not a motorcycle club or a gang of criminals, as most people think. Every one of us found something we were missing in our lives. For some it was simply a roof over their head, for others it may have been a purpose, for most it was a family."

"I don't understand. How could they find family with a bunch of strangers?"

"That's exactly what you don't understand. We didn't come into the club as strangers. We call each other brothers for a reason. We do that because we *are* brothers – we share a bond stronger than blood. There is a loyalty amongst us that most people can't even begin to imagine. Every one of my brothers and their ladies has suffered in one way or another. Some have even suffered true horrors, horrors that someone like you could never imagine. Outside the club, they have nothing. But inside the club the brotherhood brings them together and provides safety, protection, and loyalty. Every brother in this club would die for another."

He was so passionate and profound. I still didn't fully understand, most likely because I had never experienced the type of family he was describing. Don't get me wrong, I loved my parents and I knew they loved me, but the passion these men had for each other was overwhelming. It was unlike anything I had ever known. "So, how do I fit in to all of this? Why would I receive the same 'loyalty', as you put it, as, say, you would? You guys don't know me or anything about me, except for what Ice may have told you."

"Emma, listen and listen carefully. Ice's family is my family. My family is this club, just like every other brother in the club. So, if Ice says you're family, then you are family. It's just that simple. And this isn't because Ice specifically said you are family. It would be the same thing if a prospect introduced his old lady to the club. She would be welcomed as part of the family too."

It was finally starting to sink in. This life was unlike anything I had ever known, and although there were parts that scared the hell out of me, I'd been witness to what he was saying. I'd seen the brotherhood on numerous occasions. "Rebel, thank you. I appreciate you explaining all this to me. I'm starting to get it now."

He glanced over to me and asked, "But do you want it?"

Did I want it? Without it, there would be no Cade in my life. He had made that perfectly clear – he was part of the club and the club was a part of him. It was all or nothing. I thought to myself for minute. *Am I wanting this because without it, I lose Cade?* The more I thought about it, I realized that no, that wasn't it. I felt like I belonged with these guys. All my life, I'd always felt that I was one step short of everything around me. But with the Knights, I didn't. Confidently, I replied, "Yes, I do." And I meant it.

We drove for another ten or fifteen minutes and then turned off the main two-lane road we were driving on onto a very narrow dirt road. We drove for several minutes up the side of a small mountain until we came to a clearing. We turned down a driveway and as we turned the bend, I saw the most charming cabin I had ever seen. I swear I'd expected a shack, but this place was absolutely adorable.

The outside had a huge front porch, with four large rocking chairs like the ones you see at Cracker Barrel. I loved those chairs. Suddenly, I was excited to be here.

CHAPTER 24

Caden

About an hour after I texted Emma, I received a text from Rebel that they had arrived at the cabin. Finally, I could relax. Now, if I could just get through the next few days, I'd be ok.

Around 2:30, Ryder arrived with Peyton. I had been so worried about Emma that I had almost forgotten that she was coming. Good, now that I know that Emma is safe, I could talk with this girl with a clear head. I instructed Ryder to take her to my office and told them to wait for me. I rounded up Hawk, got myself a drink, and headed to the office.

"Afternoon, Ms. Anderson. I'm Ice, President of the MC. Ultimately, I am your employer. I had Ryder bring you here 'cause I wanted to ask you a few questions. You up for that?"

"Sure," she replied, cracking her gum. Damn, I hated when people did that. It grated on my nerves like fingernails on a chalkboard. I walked over to my desk and picked up an ashtray and took it over to her.

"Thanks, but I don't smoke."

Shaking my head, I replied, "It's not for you to have a smoke. It's for you to throw your gum away."

"Oh, why didn't you say so?" She quickly removed her gum and threw it away in the ashtray.

"Peyton – it is ok if I call you Peyton?" I asked. She nodded and I continued, "How long have you been working at Kandi's?"

"I guess about a year and a half." She looked around nervously and then added, "Hey, am I in some kind of trouble?"

"Not at the moment. We just need to get some information from you. If you cooperate, then you have nothing to worry about."

"Ok?" she replied hesitantly. I knew she was scared. I tried to reassure her, but I needed answers and being Mr. Nice Guy was not on my agenda at the moment. Lives were at stake and this chick was the key to saving them.

I looked over to Hawk and he nodded. He was thinking the same thing that I was: let's just cut the small talk and get to the point. "Peyton, I want you to tell me what you know about Mark Grayson."

The look that came across her face was not what I was expecting. What I had expected to see was indifference. But what I saw before me was a woman who was terrified just by the mere mention of his name. Damn, this guy must be a real piece of work. She fidgeted in her chair and finally spoke. "Oh God, did he send you after me? I swear, I never told a soul. I swear on my son!" Holy shit, she has a kid.

Hawk chimed in, "Peyton, calm down, sweetheart. Grayson did not send us after you." Hawk glanced over to me and I nodded, encouraging him to go on. "We are after Grayson."

Surprised, she looked up to Hawk. "You're after him? I thought you guys were that motorcycle club that protects him. You know, Knights of Satan, or something like that."

I turned around and showed her the patch on the back of my cut. Hawk said, "Do you see anything on there that refers to Satan?"

"No," she whispered.

Hawk continued, "That's because we are the Knights of Silence. The club you are referring to is the Satans Rebels, and they are very different from us. And yes, we know they are protecting Grayson. That's why we need your help." He paused for a moment then continued. "You see, we have found a connection between you and Grayson. We know about the trial and we know what you did. What we don't know is why. That is where you come in. You tell us the whole story, the club will offer you and your son our full protection."

"Really?" she asked, surprised. She glanced at me as if questioning Hawk's words, and I nodded as confirmation that what he was telling her was true.

"Really," I said with confidence. I wanted to make her understand that we weren't the bad guys. "Peyton, I know when you look at us, at this clubhouse, you see bikers. Your immediate thought is bad news. I get that. We all have a bad rap because of some that show no respect. For us, it's different. We respect civilians. Have we done what you would consider bad things? Yes. I'm not gonna lie to you. I've put a good many people in the ground. I have no regrets or remorse for that. They were violent, evil, disrespecting assholes. Those men made a living from the abuse of others. We have zero tolerance for that sort of shit." I paused for a moment to let her take this all in. Then, I continued, "What it comes down to is bad guys killing even worse guys. And if someone hurts one of our own ... well, I am sure you can figure out the outcome of that. The only time we involve a civilian is if it's biker business, like now. But I can assure you, nobody in this club or affiliated with this club wants to hurt you."

She was silent for a moment, then asked, "May I have a drink?"

"Sure," I replied, then I turned toward the door, opened it, and called out, "Dbag, bring the Jack and three glasses." He immediately got up off the couch and headed over to the bar.

Within five minutes, our drinks were delivered. As Dbag was about to leave, I said, "Hey, thanks. Why don't you stick around?" He nodded and took a seat next to Peyton. I poured us all a drink and asked Dbag if he wanted one, which he refused. The kid wasn't much of a drinker ... how he ended up in this crowd, I will never know. I handed Peyton and Hawk theirs and we downed them.

"Ok, I'll tell you what I know." She took a deep breath and then continued, "I met Mark Grayson six years ago. We met in a bar and hit it off. We started dating. We dated for ten months before I turned up pregnant. Mark was angry, but we decided to get married and do right by our child. A week before our wedding, Mark became convinced that the child I was carrying was not his.

He went into a jealous rage and beat the living shit out of me. After he was done using me as a punching bag, he apologized and rushed me to the hospital. He made me swear not to tell them what he'd done. He made up a story that I was mugged and he'd found me outside my apartment like this. I was sure they didn't believe me, or Mark for that matter. But no questions were asked. I almost lost my child. But by the grace of God, my son was born prematurely – but he survived.

"The last thing I wanted was to be married to an animal like that. So, I postponed the wedding. My excuse to Mark was that I didn't want to get married until Tommy (that's my son) was out of the woods and home from the hospital. Surprisingly, he agreed. The day Tommy was released from the hospital, I ran. I took my son, every penny I had saved, packed one suitcase, and left. I bought train tickets, bus tickets, and airline tickets, all going different places. I rented cars in 10 states, 9 of which I never stepped foot in. I did not want to be found."

She motioned for another drink and I poured her one and handed it to her. She downed it, set her glass on my desk, and continued. "I had a friend who created identities, and I purchased one for me and my son. For four years, I was left alone. I thought I had done it. Then, one day, Tommy and I were coming home from the store, and sitting on our front porch was Mark. I thought I was going to lose it right then and there, but knew I had to be strong for Tommy's sake. When we got to the porch, he said, 'I need your help. We need to talk.' He then turned and just walked into my house. I was shocked that he'd just walked into my house. I was sure that I'd left it locked. I found out later that he owned my house. All those years, he knew exactly where I was. And you know what the kicker was? He never even acknowledged Tommy. His flesh and blood little boy, and he couldn't even look at him. What kind of man does that?

"That was the day that I found out that he needed a key witness in a case. He told me that I had to testify to the identity of a murderer to help him win a case. I refused. That was a huge mistake. I should have known better. After I received another beating from him, he told me that if I didn't help him with this, he would make sure that my son – not his son, my son – would not live to see his fifth birthday. At that point, he knew he had me. Whether he meant it or was just bluffing, I was not going to risk my son's life. But I truly doubt that he was bluffing. It was not until I walked in to that courtroom that I found out who he was defending."

I could not believe what I was hearing. This Grayson guy was truly fucked up. The thought that Emma could've married this asshole made my stomach turn. Thank fuck that was not gonna happen. "Peyton, honey, what happened after you testified?"

"Grayson said I needed to stay in Pennsylvania. He said he may get to know his son again, which I had assumed was a scare tactic. After what he had done to me, I realized what kind of man he was. He would be the last person I would want to be in my son's life. That alone was enough to scare me enough to do what he had asked. He said that if I ran again, he would be able to find me just as easily as he had before. So, here I was, back home, with a kid and no job. About two days later, Grayson called and said that Kandi's was looking to hire a bartender. I'd had experience tending bar, and nothing else was panning out. My mom was able to watch Tommy in the evenings, and I could be there to get him to school and pick him up after. It seemed like the perfect solution. I was hired, and six months ago I decided to start dancing. More money, if you know what I mean."

I looked over to Hawk. "That son of a bitch planted her there."

Hawk replied, "It is sure looking that way. Question is, now what do we do?"

I looked back to Peyton. "Is there anything else you can tell us? Anything – the smallest thing could be significant."

She hesitated for a moment, then shook her head. "Nah, I really can't think of anything."

"Well if you do, will you let us know? You can get to one of us through Callie at the club."

"Sure." She got up to leave and then asked, "How am I going to get back?"

"Give us a minute. Why don't you have a seat at the bar out there and I'll have Dbag give you a ride back to the club." She

162

started to walk out of my office when I remembered I needed to remind her of something very important. I called after her, "Peyton." She turned to face me. "I know this goes without saying, but you are not to talk about this meeting with anyone. Not even Callie. Understood?"

"Understood. And you promise that my son and I will be safe?"

"I do. Just make sure nobody knows that we have met or that you have been to the clubhouse."

"Ok." She turned to leave.

When she closed the door behind her, I looked over to Hawk. "I want two guys on her and her son. Keep her safe."

"You got it, chief. Now back to my question, what are we gonna do about this?"

I shook my head. "Fuck if I know. You boys got any suggestions?"

"Boss, I think we should do nothing," Hawk replied.

Confused, I looked up to him and asked, "What's your thinking behind that?"

He sat down in the chair that Peyton had just vacated, leaned forward and said, "Hear me out. If we do something now, we lose the advantage. If we do something, then Grayson and the Satans know we know that Peyton is a plant. She may be a plant that they haven't used yet, but she is still in place for when they need her. With all this going on, they are gonna need her real soon and my guess is that she will need to get an 'in' with the club. Why don't we give her one before they ask?"

"Wouldn't that give her away?" I asked.

"Not if she is dating one of the brothers," he replied.

Holy shit, he was on to something. We both turned toward Dbag. "No, no, no ... guys, come on. Don't make me do this. I mean hell, she's hot and all, but I just met her today," Dbag pleaded.

Hawk and I started to laugh. "Look at it this way, you might actually get some pussy."

He turned away in disgust, mumbling under his breath, "You guys are sick."

Hawk was still laughing and then said, "Go out there and get your girl, we need to tell her about the new love of her life." We both broke out into hysterics. I really didn't know what was so funny about all this, but it felt good to laugh. All this shit had been going on too long. I truly didn't believe Dbag had been with a chick before. We'd never seen him with any of the sweetbutts. He spent more time with his computers and surveillance equipment. He was such a freaking nerd, but he was invaluable to the club.

Dbag came back with Peyton, who looked upset again. "I thought we were done?" she asked.

"We were, but now we need your help with something," I stated.

She walked over to the chair and sat down, defeated. "What?" she asked exasperated, as if she was saying, "*What else do you guys want from me?*"

"Peyton, like I said before, if word gets out that you and I have spoken, your life and your son's life will be in danger. So, I am going to have two men watching you both at all times."

Relieved, she said, "Thank you."

She started to get up to leave when I added, "There's more."

"Oh?"

"We are convinced that Grayson and the Satans told you about this job to use you as a plant against the Knights," I said.

She immediately chimed in, "But they haven't asked me to do anything – just to not leave the area. I swear!" She was starting to get a little hysterical.

"Peyton, calm down, please. We know that. But that does not mean that they won't be asking you to get them intel on the club. If that's the case, you will need to be 'in' with the club. Do you understand what I mean?"

"I'm guessing that I'll need a reason to hang out at the clubhouse. Something that would be airtight," she said. I was impressed; I'd expected a dumb brunette, but she was a smart cookie. I guess with what she had been through, she would have to be.

"Exactly. We came up with a plan that will work like a charm. You are gonna start dating Dbag here." I slapped him on the back and lightly pushed him toward her.

"But ... I can't," she protested.

Dbag chimed in and said, "See, I told you, this isn't going to work. She doesn't want to do it any more than I do." He was desperate. I felt bad for the kid, but we would have never asked him if we didn't need him. And he knew that too.

"Look you two, I don't have time for this. Dbag, take Peyton back to work. If you two are having relationship problems, work it out. I'm not a dating counselor."

Knowing that he had no other choice, Dbag reached for Peyton's arm and guided her out of the office. "Come on Peyton, let's get you back to work," he said, defeated. She started to protest, but soon realized that we weren't going to budge on this.

As they left my office, Hawk and I burst out laughing.

CHAPTER 25

Emma

Rebel and I carried all the packages and my bags inside. The inside of the cabin was just as charming as the outside. Not the best of furnishings, but still much more homey than I'd expected. This place would make a great romantic getaway for Caden and me. A smile came across my face while my brain faded off into dreamland.

"Hey, you ok?" Rebel stirred me from my fantasies as he walked past me and dropped the bags he was carrying on the kitchen counter.

"Yeah, I'm good. Just thinking." My voice faded for a moment, and then I said, "Leave those. I'll put the food away. It's the least I can do since you did all the driving."

"Not going to argue with you there, darlin'." He smiled and plopped himself down on the couch, taking out his phone. I assumed that he had a girlfriend of some sort, or perhaps even an old lady that he was texting.

"Checking in with your girl?" I asked.

"Naw, ain't got one of those. Just letting Ice know we're here and all is good."

As I started to put the groceries away, I figured this was a good opportunity to find out more about my protector. "So, why no girl? Haven't found the right one yet?"

He chuckled. "Oh I found the right one, she just hasn't figured that out yet. But someday, she will." He said it as if he completely believed it. Good for him. I wonder who it is. Maybe I have met her. "Do I know her?"

"Now, Emma, don't you go worrying your pretty little head about my love life."

I should have known he wasn't going to tell me. So, I decided to change the subject to something I knew he would talk about. "So, what would you like for dinner tonight?"

Ah, the mention of food perked him up quick. He sat up and said, "How about we grill those steaks. It's a nice night."

That sounded awesome. "You got it," I replied. I finished putting away the groceries and checking out the kitchen – if I was going to cook, I had to know my way around. After I got everything put up and familiarized myself with my surroundings, I was tired. I wanted to speak to Caden and then take a nap. I worried about him as much as he worried about me.

I looked over to Rebel and he was sound asleep on the couch. So, I guessed I was going to explore on my own. As I stepped into the great room from the kitchen, to the left I could see large glass patio doors that lead to a nice-sized patio. I walked over to look out and saw a whole other kitchen and living room out there. All open, with screens that could be pulled down if needed. It was beautiful. I turned back toward the inside of the house and walked past the floor-to-ceiling stone fireplace and headed toward the stairs. "*Hell, with the right furnishings and décor, this place could be gorgeous,*" I thought to myself.

I proceeded up the twisting, turning spiral staircase to see what was up there. It lead to a loft that overlooked the great room. I hadn't noticed that before. I peeked over the rail and saw that Rebel was still asleep on the couch. I guess our early departure was a little too early for him. As I walked down the hall, I noticed several bedrooms that lined the perimeter of the loft. I peeked into the first room: no bed. It was fair to assume that this was not going to be my room. The next bedroom had Rebel's duffle on the bed, so I was guessing that he had claimed that room. After checking two more rooms, I finally found my bags in the nicest room of them all.

Wow, this room was gorgeous. The furnishings were very masculine, and I think it was fair to assume this was most likely Caden's room. Was this Caden's house? Where did he get the money for a place like this?

Just as I was placing my bags on the dresser to free up the bed, I heard a beep coming from my purse. That damn new phone. I will never get used to that ringtone. I need to change it to something that's more familiar. When I got to the phone, it was ringing. The number that showed up on the caller ID was the same number that Caden had been texting me from, so I was sure it was safe to answer.

"Hello?"

"Hey, beautiful. How's my girl?" I heard the sweet sound of Caden's voice through the phone. Relief washed over me.

"Oh Caden, I'm good. But, I miss you."

His low baritone chuckle warmed my heart. Then he said, "Sweetheart, it's only been a few hours."

He was right. I was being ridiculous. "I know, you are right," I said sheepishly.

"So are you all settled in?" he then asked.

"Yes, Rebel carried in the bags and groceries and I put everything away. He's taking a nap on the couch, and I was thinking about doing the same."

He interrupted, "Wait, what did you just say?"

Confused, I answered, "Rebel's asleep, and ..." Before I could finish, Caden began yelling into the phone.

"What the hell, you guys just got there and he's already sleeping!? Emma, put that asshole on the phone!" Oh boy, he's mad now. But he's about to get even more mad.

"No!"

"Emma, don't you tell me no. He's there to watch you, and he can't do that through his fucking eyelids! Damnit, now wake his ass up and put him on the phone!"

It was a good thing that Caden wasn't here and we were having this conversation over the phone. He was being unfair to Rebel, and I was not going to allow it. If he was here, I probably would not win this argument, but since he was not, I was proud to say that I would be the victor. "Caden Jackson, now you listen to me! That man just spent the last several hours driving me up here to God knows where. He deserves some rest. He is sound asleep on the couch, and I will not wake him. Calm down, we are just fine. Besides, like I told you, I was just thinking about taking a nap myself. Someone kept me up pretty late last night, and then woke me up too early this morning," I said teasingly.

I expected more anger, but what I got instead surprised me. He chuckled into the phone and then said, "Oh baby, just you wait until I get up there. You better get used to that bed you are sleeping in, 'cause I plan on keeping you there for a long time. And sweetheart, don't think I am letting your little lecture slide, you will pay for that too!" The way he said this gave me goosebumps, and I could feel the wetness pool between my legs.

I had to change the subject. "So, how are things going in Edinboro?"

"Good," he said.

"Is that all you are going to tell me?"

"Emma, we talked about this," he said, frustrated.

"I know, we did, but you said we could discuss this stuff when you weren't in front of the others. It's so hard being kept in the dark, Caden. I'm trying, really."

"I know baby, I know you are. Maybe if you look at it this way: in all likelihood, the less you know, the safer you are."

"That makes no sense."

"It does to me. Emma, you have to understand that there are some things you cannot know, even when we are alone. If you ask about something and I can tell you, I will. Just know we have this rule to keep our women safe. If you cannot accept this, then this won't work between us. I need to know babe, you in or out?"

"Caden, is that question really necessary? In the last two weeks my life has done a complete 180. I've broken my engagement, found out that the man I was engaged to is a complete psychopath, and you came back into my life. Plus I'll probably lose my job, since I cannot use my computer and I have no means of getting my bills paid or things taken care of in my day-to-day life that need to be done. So I ask you, do you think any of that matters to me if it means that I can ultimately be with you? I told you before; I've loved you as long as I can remember. Yes, there are things you can't tell me – I don't like it, but I am learning to accept it. Why? Because, I trust you, Caden, and I believe in you." Maybe he would finally understand that I was in this for the long haul and I was not running.

"And what about my club?" he asked hesitantly.

I giggled into the phone, "They're growing on me?"

He laughed. I guess he liked that response. He then added, "Well beautiful, I better go. I'll check in with you tomorrow. Don't make any outgoing calls, and don't call this number unless it is an absolute emergency. Something goes wrong, you call me. You got it?"

"Ok." I was a little bummed that I could not call him if I just wanted to talk to him. But, I understood.

"And Emma," he added. "You don't answer this phone for any number except this one."

"Ok." He was quickly going from boyfriend mode to president of the MC mode, but all I wanted to hear was how much he missed me. Oh well ... he carried a lot on his shoulders, and I knew he was worried about me.

"Well, I better go. Talk to you tomorrow?"

"Sure." I was trying not to cry, but for some reason I was feeling very emotional. Hopefully he did not know that I was upset. It was silly, and I really didn't want to explain myself.

"Bye, beautiful," he said. Good, he didn't know. Unless he'd just chosen to ignore it. That would have been the guy thing to do.

"Bye, Caden."

Just as I was about to hang up the phone I heard, "Hey," coming through the speaker.

"Yeah?" I asked eagerly.

"I miss you, baby."

What a relief! "I miss you too!" And then he hung up.

Once I laid myself down, it was not long before I fell asleep.

CHAPTER 26

Caden

Three days later I was hanging out at the clubhouse when Dbag came in and said he had some news. It appears that we were right about Grayson. According to what Dbag reported, Grayson had made contact with Peyton. He had told Peyton that he'd heard that she had hooked up with one of the Knights. And just like we had expected, he asked her to let him know what was going on with our club. It was exactly what we wanted. Now we could feed bogus information to her and back it up. Then when we were ready to make our move, the Satans would be exactly where we wanted them.

It was time for church. We needed to discuss strategy and vote on a plan.

Let the games begin.

Two hours later, all the boys had arrived. All except Rebel, but he was on a more important mission.

I called the meeting to order and we went over some general business. Cash reported that the club had over 50k in the bank and that Ryder still owed his dues for this month. Hawk reported that he had seen a Satan driving down Waterford St. We all agreed that it was very odd for any Satan to be seen in the city limits of Edinboro. They usually kept to the outskirts of our town, avoiding a direct confrontation with the Knights.

Once the general business was out of the way, I spoke up. "Now let's get to the matter at hand." I explained to the club what we'd found out over the last few days: the connection between Grayson and the Satans, and the situation with Peyton and Dbag. "What we need to figure out now is what are we gonna feed to Peyton that we want to get back to Grayson. The Satans may be our enemies, but I am convinced that Grayson is running the show. He has gotten these boys off time and time again; they owe him. If he says jump, I'm sure their response is 'how high?' So, we need to provide intel that pans out so that they trust the rest of the information she is feeding them. Anyone got any ideas?" I looked around the room, waiting for something. They all looked all around to each other.

Finally, Spike spoke up. "We could set up a phony deal, perhaps a protection run at the docks. Pull in some guys from other Chapters to pose as the dealers who are selling their product. Do you think they will immediately act?"

Shaking my head, I said, "No, I don't believe so. They will wait until there is an opportunity to take us all down, and they will make sure that I am there. For some reason that I did not understand, Grayson has a personal grudge against me." I paused for a moment and then added, "I believe they will check us out first. If we send two guys and we use two guys from another Chapter, it won't be worth the risk for them to make their move."

Hawk agreed, "You are exactly right, Ice. I don't see them making any more moves until they think they are hitting the jackpot."

The others agreed. I said, "I'll contact our Chapter in Lexington. They are far enough away that they won't recognize them as our own. Ok, boys, so that's one. What else?" Some of the guys threw a couple other ideas on the table, but nothing seemed to click.

"Why does it have to be a deal?" Hawk asked. "Why can't we just feed to them that we are having a special party? You know, a family deal. We can easily do it, and it will be another bit of intel that will check out."

"I don't know," I responded. "There has to be a draw, something they want."

"What about Emma?"

Quickly shaking my head, I responded, "No. She isn't safe here."

Hawk pleaded, "Ice, that's not what I am saying. All the brothers, their old ladies, kids, and sweetbutts will be here. They won't risk taking down the clubhouse, not with woman and kids here. I know they don't have the same values as we do, but I am pretty confident that they don't want any collateral damage of women and children in a club war. But, it will convince them that Emma is under our protection." He took a breath and then continued, "I am convinced that they know we have moved Emma. I don't know if they know for sure where she is, but if they see her here, they will think we brought her back and won't be looking for her elsewhere."

I was confused. "Hawk, I'm not following you. We would still have to bring Emma back, wouldn't we?"

He smiled. "No, that's the beauty of it. From a distance, another tall, leggy girl with long blonde hair could be Emma. No disrespect to your old lady, boss, but we could plant a decoy. The only catch is that she would have to be *your girl* for the night."

"How in the hell are we gonna pull that off?" I had a bad feeling about this. There were so many things that could go wrong. "Besides, who do we got that could step in as Emma?"

"Honey," Hawk stated. All the guys nodded in agreement. Shit. I could see it working with Honey, but did I really want to go there just to convince the Satans that Emma was here? And more importantly, how would Emma take it? Should I tell her? I shouldn't agree to this, I knew that, but five minutes later I found myself agreeing to the plan.

As the boys were leaving, I asked Hawk to send in Honey. I might as well get this part over and done with. Five minutes later, Honey was closing the door behind her.

"Hawk said you needed to see me, Ice?" Honey asked.

"Yeah, why don't you have a seat?" She gingerly sat down and looked up to me with curious concern. "Honey, you've been a part of this club now for many years. You've been loyal to the club and that has not gone unnoticed. You are an asset to this club and every brother loves you. You have cleaned up our bloody messes, our drunken brawls, and have made sure we have decent meals to eat."

She interrupted hesitantly, "Ice, have I done something wrong?" Shit, I was not going about this the right way. The last thing I wanted her to think was that she had done something wrong. I'd thought that if I brought out her good points, I'd be pumping her up, letting her know how much we appreciate her. But, instead, it has backfired. Now she thinks she is in trouble.

"Honey, no, it's nothing like that." I tried to reassure her, but she had that look. You know, the one that says, *"The last thing I want to do is disappoint you."* I said, "What I am getting at is that we have never involved you in club business. We never wanted to. Not because we didn't trust you, but because we didn't want you to get hurt. But unfortunately, the time has come that the club needs you."

She sighed, obviously relieved. "You know I would do anything for the club. I came to you beaten and broken, and you and the club took me in. You gave me a roof over my head, a home, and more importantly, a family. You just name it, I'll do it."

"You might not feel that way when you hear what we need."

"Ice, just tell me. Quit beating around the bush and just spill it." That's my girl, strong and solid. Not afraid of anything.

"If you haven't noticed, you resemble Emma." Suddenly, I saw a disappointed look come across her face. I knew this part was gonna get sticky. But I had to make her understand. So, I continued without allowing her to say anything. "Emma is in danger. That's why I sent her away. But we need the Satans to think that she is still here. We need them to stop looking for her. Basically, we need a decoy. That's where you come in." She took a deep breath in anticipation for me to go on. So I did. "The boys and I think that from a distance, dressed in the right clothes – and if you straighten your hair a bit – you could be a dead ringer for Emma."

"Where will I be the decoy? Will I be in danger?" she asked.

"You'll be right here at the clubhouse. We're having a party Saturday night. We are tipping off the Satans that Emma will be here, and you just need to stand in. I cannot imagine that the Satans would make a hit on the clubhouse, especially since all the old ladies and children will be here. So, I believe you will be safe. But as both you and I know, there are no guarantees."

"Will you be with me?" she asked. Here came the hard part.

"Yes, I will."

"Why do I feel that there is more?" she asked.

"You are a smart woman, Honey. Yes, there is more." I paused, took a deep breath, and continued, "We need to be convincing. Do you know what I mean by that?"

"I think I do. But maybe you should spell it out for me. You know, so I don't make any false assumptions."

"We will need to be on display during this party. Lots of public displays of affection: kissing, perhaps even running off together leaving the assumption out there that we want to be alone. Can you do that?"

"Do I have time to think about it?" she asked.

"Unfortunately, not a lot. I can give you a couple of minutes now if that will help. I'm sorry for putting you on the spot like this, but we need to act on this quickly." I paused and then added, "I know we have some history, and I am guessing that this could be difficult for you; I don't want you hurt."

We sat in silence for about five minutes and then she said, "I'll do it."

Smiling at her, I got up from my desk and kissed her on the cheek. "You are an amazing woman, Honey. One day, one of these boys is gonna be very lucky making you their old lady."

Her eyes started to well up as she looked up to me and said, "You think so, Ice? You really think there is someone out there for me?"

Pulling her into my arms, I hugged her close. "I sure as hell do. Someone better than me."

CHAPTER 27

Caden

I contacted our Lexington Chapter. They were on board. They would be here tomorrow morning. Peyton did her part and set up Grayson with news of a protection run on a gun shipment going down tomorrow night at the docks in Erie. So far, the first part of our plan was all set.

The Lexington boys (Jagger and Snake) arrived around 10 am the next morning. Jagger was the club's VP and Snake was a prospect on his first job. We filled them in on all the details. Hawk and Ryder were gonna go from our Chapter. We loaded the boys up with a crate of guns from our personal stock, leaving the remainder of the crates in the van empty. The Satans only needed to see one of them full. It would be dark. Our boys would wear their cuts, but the Lexington boys would not. They would do the deal, bring the guns back to the clubhouse, and the Lexington boys would lay low for a day or two before coming back in. It was all set for 11:58 pm tonight. This had to work.

For the rest of the day, I kept myself busy. At 11 pm that evening the boys left and all I could do was wait. Wait for word that this worked. We sent four guys with them, hiding out watching to make sure that the Satans checked us out. Dbag was to make contact with me as soon as it all went down.

I hadn't spoken to Emma for a couple of days now, but we did text each day to just check in and to confirm with the other that we were safe. Rebel also kept me apprised of their situation on a daily basis, but that still didn't keep me from worrying about them. This whole thing with Honey tomorrow night had me on edge. At first I had planned on telling Emma, but eventually I decided against it. She was worried about enough right now, I didn't need to add more to her plate. I could worry enough for the both of us.

At 1:10 am, Dbag made contact.

> All good, the boys are coming back. Jagger and Snake headed to our safe house in Erie. Will fill you in on the details when we get back.

That was exactly what I needed to hear. My boys were whole. When they got back, they were ready to give me a full report.

"Ice, it worked like a charm," Hawk said as he closed my office door behind him.

Ryder chimed in and said, "Yeah, we had the Lexington boys pull up on a motorboat. They got out, checked the merchandise, gave their ok, and we loaded the crates on the boat and they left. In the distance, we heard bikes approaching. They slowed when they got to the dock, then sped up and left."

Dbag added, "Yeah Ice, it was awesome. I was watching from the window in the warehouse next to the dock we were using. They just did a drive-by. Their lead checked out."

I was so proud of them. They'd handled this job with the utmost professionalism. I'd expected nothing less from them, but each time something works in our favor, I can't help but feel like a proud father. "Great job, guys. Now, we just need to have this party tomorrow fly without a hitch and we've got Grayson and the Satans by the balls. Now why don't you boys get yourself a drink, wind down, and relax. We got a big night tomorrow."

They left my office and I decided to take my own advice. I closed up the office and decided to head to bed. Tomorrow night was my show. When I got myself settled in my room I looked at my watch: 2am. Shit, I really wanted to talk to Emma, but I didn't want to startle her with a late night phone call. So I sent her a text, turned off the light, and went to bed.

Goodnight beautiful. I love you.

CHAPTER 28

Emma

I woke up Saturday morning feeling surprisingly good. I had gone to bed last night with a migraine, and usually I wake up feeling the same. Rebel gave me something he had for headaches – it knocked me out, but it also made me feel better.

I laid in bed for several minutes, soaking in the sunlight that was streaming through the window. It had been a whole week since I'd seen Caden and I was missing him so much. Still, Rebel had turned out to be a good friend. Other than Caden, I've never had a male friend, especially one that I was not attracted to. Oh, don't get me wrong; Rebel is a very nice-looking guy: great body, blond hair, and hazel-green eyes. He even has a great personality to boot. I made a mental note to myself; I needed to find Rebel a nice girl.

I picked up my phone to see if I had any messages; I had just one message from Cade. He was the only one who had my phone number, so why would I think anyone else would call or message me? Besides, his was the only message I wanted.

I read his message and couldn't believe what I was seeing. He said he loves me. He really loves me. I guess I've always known it, but deep down I really wanted him to say it. And he will. Typing the words in a text was a start.

With an extra spring in my step, I showered and got ready for the day. Rebel and I didn't have any plans for today – after all, there wasn't a lot we could do up here. However, he did promise me a backgammon tournament. I was looking forward to finally beating his butt!

I came downstairs and found him cooking breakfast. Well, that was a first. "Mmmmmm, that smells wonderful," I said as I rounded into the kitchen. "Whatcha making?"

"Well good morning, sleeping beauty. It's about time you woke up." He smiled and turned toward the skillet of bacon on the stove. "I thought since you are always cooking for me, I would do something nice for you for a change."

"Awww, aren't you sweet. I don't care what those brothers of yours say about you, you are a nice guy." I walked over to him and kissed him on the cheek. "Can I help?"

"Nope, I got this under control." He paused for a moment and then with a guilty look on his face said, "Damn Emma, I can't lie to you. I was getting hungry and didn't know when you were getting up. I was tired of waiting for you and decided to give it a go."

"So the truth comes out," I said teasingly. Then I added, "Can I let you in on a little secret?"

"What?"

"I still think you are a nice guy." After I said that, I swear I saw the big bad biker blush. Mission accomplished.

When breakfast was done cooking, we sat down and ate in silence. He really did a good job, but in all honesty, how can you really screw up scrambled eggs and bacon? But I was grateful all the same.

I was helping Rebel clean up when my phone rang. Must be Cade. I ran over to it on the counter and answered, "Hello."

"Hello, beautiful. How's my best girl this morning?"

"I'm great. Rebel gave me the day off from cooking and fixed me breakfast. I cannot wait to see what he does with lunch and dinner." I said into the phone, winking at Rebel. He turned to me with a towel in his hand and twisted it and flicked it at me. It hit my leg, and I couldn't contain the pain. "Ow!" I yelled into the phone.

"What the hell, Emma? What happened?" he asked anxiously.

"It's nothing. Rebel and I were having a disagreement and he hit me." Oh no, that came out wrong. Before I could correct myself, Caden started screaming into the phone.

"What the fuck! Put Rebel on the phone! Now!" I handed the phone to Rebel and mouthed the words "sorry" as he took the phone. I could hear Caden yelling through the phone, but I couldn't make out what he was saying. Rebel was giving short answers: "Yes, sir," and "You got it, Prez."

Then I heard, "No boss, it's not what you think. I would never lay a hand on your girl, I swear." More yelling from Caden and then, "She is in good hands. I would never let you down." Caden seemed to calm down after that. I didn't hear his yelling anymore, but he was still talking. Rebel was nodding and saying, "Mmhmm," but gave no indication that I could make out as to what they were talking about. He said goodbye and handed the phone back to me.

"Caden?" Nothing, the phone was dead. He hung up and didn't even say goodbye to me. I looked up to Rebel and asked, "Did he hang up?"

"Yep, he had to go."

Sadly I asked, "Didn't he want to talk to me anymore?" I hadn't spoken to him in several days now, and all I got was a hello this morning and he was gone. Something was going on, I just knew it.

"I told you princess, he had to go. It's all good. Don't worry. He's got a party to get ready for tonight."

"Party?" He was having a party tonight without me? With all this mess going on, why in the hell was he having a party?

"Club business, sweetheart. Remember, it's on a need-to-know basis," he smugly reminded me. Suddenly, I didn't like him anymore. Well, I did, but I hated the fact that he knew more than I did. Men! Sometimes I think they are worthless creatures that God put on this earth to merely torture us. But I loved that worthless creature who was having a party tonight without me, even though I was extremely jealous that I wouldn't be there. But I didn't say any more about it. I refused to give Rebel any inclination that this whole party thing bothered me. Especially since I was sure that he would tell Caden.

I spent the remainder of the day reading. I didn't feel like being social and Rebel watched TV all day. Before I knew it, it was after 9 pm and my eyes were heavy. My first thought was that the party would be starting soon. Why did I have such an uneasy feeling about this? Something had been nagging at me all day about this party, but I couldn't pinpoint what was actually bothering me: just not being there, or something totally different and much, much worse.

I had texted Caden throughout the day, but he never responded. That didn't help matters. Why was he avoiding me? Had something changed between us? I needed to stop this. I was worrying about this stuff as if I were a seventeen-year-old girl with her first real boyfriend. Enough is enough. I got up out of the chair and said to Rebel, "Goodnight, I'm going to bed."

I heard him say "Goodnight" as I was heading up the stairs.

I checked my phone one last time before I turned out the light. Nothing. For the first time since I left the clubhouse with Rebel, I felt scared.

CHAPTER 29

Caden

Today was crazy. It all started with that phone call to Emma. What the hell was going on with her and Rebel? I trust Rebel, I really do, and I believe him when he said that there was nothing going on. But fuck, why was it still bothering me? I had meant to text Emma several times today. But every time I received a text from her, I wasn't in a position that I could respond immediately. Then I would get immersed into something else and forget about it. Now the party was about to start and I had to keep my head. Tonight is too important.

Honey and I checked out Emma's room and luckily, she'd left a few things behind. We found a pair of skinny jeans and a simple black shirt and black boots. Perfect. And everything fit perfect. Honey looked uncomfortable; she wasn't used to wearing clothes that covered her up so much. After she took the clothes, she went back to her room to finish getting ready. As she walked out the door, I reminded her, "Don't forget, no curls tonight. Straight."

She turned back at me and gave me a look and said, "I know, Ice. Relax, I got this."

I nodded and she left.

The party started early with the kids. We cooked out, the kids played, and everything was going perfectly. Except, where was Honey? She had yet to emerge from her room and I was getting worried. I was constantly checking my watch, expecting her at any minute. But to no avail; she did not come down.

Around 8 pm, she finally decided to show herself. As she came down the stairs, which were on the other side of the room from where I was standing, I noticed that she really did look like Emma. The resemblance was uncanny. She walked directly over to me, kissed me on the cheek, and said, "Ready to get this party started?"

I smiled and said, "Let's do it." We started to walk outside so we could be seen, since most of the attendees were already enjoying the pleasant spring evening. I leaned over to her and whispered, "You look great!"

She beamed and said, "Thanks!"

I had guys positioned in the hills around the clubhouse so that they could check and make sure that we were being watched. Around 10:45, I received a text from Ryder. The Satans were watching. Great. I leaned in to Honey and whispered in her ear, "Show time. You ready for this?" She nodded and I immediately pulled her close. I nuzzled her neck and gave her light kisses behind her ear. She giggled.

We walked over to some other brothers and their old ladies hanging around the portable bar we'd placed outside. We talked with them for a while and then Honey turned toward me and slid her arms up my torso and latched them behind my neck. I hesitated for a minute, and she just looked at me, reminding me what we were doing this for. I didn't care. I knew it was for a good reason, but every part of me felt like I was cheating on Emma. Thank fuck she will never know about this. I leaned in and kissed Honey. It wasn't Emma's kiss, and I felt horrible afterward ... but I did what I had to do to keep her safe. If she ever does find out, hopefully she will understand.

We carried on like a couple who were very much in love. As time passed it became increasingly hard for me to put on this show. Finally around 11:45, Honey and I decided to make our departure and head for the bedroom as planned. About 15 minutes after we left, Ryder sent me a text and said that the Satans had left. We were clear and the charade was over.

"Honey, we're good. The Satans left. You can head back to your room now."

Disappointed, she replied, "Ok, if you don't need anything else."

As she walked toward the door I called after her, "Hey." She turned to me and I continued, "You did great tonight. I know this wasn't easy for you. Thanks!"

She smirked and said, "Unfortunately, Ice, it was a lot easier than I thought." She stepped toward the door and then added, "But it's over now. Goodnight, Ice. Sleep well."

Damnit. I'd known this was going to hurt her. Why had I agreed to this? For Emma, that's why. I had to do it for Emma. I had to keep reminding myself of that. The good news is that the Satans and Grayson think Emma is here, so I won't be followed anymore. I was now free to make a road trip to Rome to see my girl.

The next morning, Honey and a couple of prospects were cleaning up the mess from last night's party. Hell, we could be a bunch of slobs. I went to get some coffee and headed for my office. We had to plan the final takedown – it wasn't gonna happen by itself. I texted Hawk, Ryder, Dbag, and Spike; I had an idea that I wanted to run by them before I presented it to the whole club.

> Meeting in 30. Being hungover is not an excuse for your absence.

I could be such a dick. But shit needed to get done, and I had to make sure it happened.

Thirty minutes later, the boys were in the chapel waiting for me. I walked into the room and started the meeting. "So it looks like the two plants worked and the Satans bought them. We now have to figure out our next move. We need to stay on top of this. I'm thinking that we want their clubhouse empty, or at least as empty as it can get. We get them to go somewhere, maybe feed them a gun deal that's too sweet for them to resist, then we raid the clubhouse and get Brianne out. I don't have all the details figured out yet, but what do you all think?"

"We have to get Brianne out. There is no question about that, and I agree, it will be better to make that move when the clubhouse isn't quite so full of Satans," Hawk responded. "But, we'll only have a short time to get in and get out. We need to send them far enough away that their travel time is enough to make our move. Once they realize that we set them up, they will come back at us with everything they have."

Ryder added, "Are we ready for that?"

I shrugged. "We're gonna have to be. If we are gonna get Brianne out and keep Emma safe, we gotta do this. Agreed?"

"Agreed," said Ryder.

"Agreed," said Hawk.

"I'm in," Dbag added.

"Count me in, too!" said Spike.

"Ok, let's spend the rest of today working out the details. This has to be perfect. No mistakes. We can present it to the club at Church tomorrow." The boys agreed, and for the next several hours we worked up a plan to get the Satans away from their clubhouse and for us to go in and rescue Brianne. By the time we were done, we were all pleased with what we had come up. We all realized that we could not act right away and had to put the operation off for a week or so, but all of us were sure this would work.

After Church tomorrow, I was taking a much-needed vacation.

Church was scheduled for 10 am the next morning. Everyone was in attendance, except of course for Rebel. We even invited Jagger and Snake from the Lexington Chapter. They were sticking around in case we needed them, and we felt it was important to include them in on our plan.

I called the meeting to order. After we discussed general business, our focus went to keeping Emma safe and rescuing Brianne. "Boys, as you all know, we have spent the last couple of days feeding information to the Satans. We wanted them to trust our mole, and it appears that it has worked. Now it is time for us to move forward and get Emma's friend out. Some of the boys and I met yesterday, and we came up with a plan that we think will work. I'll spend the next several minutes going over those details with you all. I would appreciate it if you hold your comments until I am done. Understood?"

Everyone nodded in agreement and I then continued, "The gist of the plan is to raid the Satans' clubhouse, rescue Brianne, and then blow it up. Keep in mind that I don't want any civilian casualties, so we will have to be very careful to ensure that we get everyone out." I paused for a moment and looked at my brothers, who all looked confused. I'd expected as much. "I know you all are wondering how we are gonna accomplish this. Well, this is what we intend to do ..."

By the time I was done going over all the details, the boys were pumped. They wanted to act right away, but I explained to them that we had to wait. If this was going to work, it had to be done at the right time. Timing was everything.

I ended the meeting telling my boys to spend the next several days with their families. I explained to them that I was heading out of town for a few days and that we just needed to lay low for now. They all agreed.

After the meeting adjourned, I texted Rebel and told him that I was tying up loose ends here and that I would be heading his way. I asked him not to tell Emma; I wanted to surprise her. Two hours later, I was on my Harley heading to Rome.

CHAPTER 30

Emma

I didn't hear from Caden all night last night. I'm sure he was too busy at the party. I couldn't figure out what was going on, but I knew something was up. But I was not going to contact him again. If he wanted to talk to me, he knew where to find me. I knew it was childish, but I was not the one going to a party without him.

After cleaning up the breakfast dishes and putting things away, I noticed that we were running low on food. "Rebel, we need to make a grocery run today."

"Already?"

I laughed. "You like to eat," I reminded him.

"Hey," he said. "I'm a big boy. I need my nourishment."

I laughed harder. He had a point. Something had to fuel all that muscle. "So, can you take me to the market, or can I take the car?" I knew the answer, but it didn't hurt to ask – maybe I'd get lucky and get some alone time.

"I'll take you. You know Ice's rules." That was the response I was expecting. However, it still didn't stop my disappointment. It would have been nice to just do something on my own. It's been two weeks, and except for when I am sleeping or showering, Rebel has been my constant shadow.

About an hour later, we were getting ready to leave for the market. At least the change of scenery would be nice; I was looking forward to getting away from the house for an hour or so. We drove back the way we came and stopped at the same market we'd stopped at on the way here. It must be the only one around, and it wasn't close or convenient.

Rebel followed me into the store. I was carrying my list, preoccupied with what I needed to get and definitely not paying attention to what was going on around me. I headed over to the produce section when I accidentally bumped into someone. Looking up, I said, "I'm so sorry. I wasn't paying attention."

He nodded and said, "No problem, ma'am." As he turned away, I noticed that he had a devil tattoo on the back of his neck. His shirt covered most of it, but I could definitely make out the horns and the ominous satanic face. I felt that I had seen that picture before, but couldn't place it.

After the man walked away, Rebel came up behind me and said, "Everything ok?"

Still a little disoriented by my encounter, I replied, "Yeah, sure. I just bumped into that gentleman over there." I pointed in the direction that the man had headed, but he was gone. It was if he'd just disappeared. "That's weird."

"What?" Rebel asked.

Confused, I replied, "There was a man ... but he's gone now."

"Emma, what man? What happened?" Rebel asked, concerned. I could see the worry in his eyes and hear it in his voice. The man with the tattoo was probably nothing ... but now the hair on the back of my neck began to prickle and I could feel that we were being watched.

"At first I thought it was nothing, but there was this man that I bumped into. I said I was sorry and when he turned to leave, I noticed a devil tattoo on the back of his neck. When I went to point him out to you, he just disappeared. Rebel, what's going on? I'm scared."

Trying to reassure me, Rebel said, "It'll be ok. Just don't go wandering off and stick with me. We need to hurry up and get done with this shopping and get you back to the house." He was worried. Bless his heart for trying to make me feel better. However, it didn't work.

We finished our shopping and loaded our groceries into the car. As we pulled out of the parking lot, we noticed a single Harley parked near the front of the store. Rebel kept his eyes on the road and said, "Keep your eyes on that bike over there. If you see someone come out and get on, tell me." I did, but nobody got on the bike. We were safe – for now.

We got back to the house and Rebel and I proceeded to carry our groceries in. At one point Rebel was in the house and I was heading out to the car to get another load when I got that same uneasy feeling I'd had in the grocery store. Someone was watching me. I could feel it.

I leaned in to get another load and just as I was turning to head to the house with the bags, my body was slammed against the car, a cloth was put over my face, and everything went black.

My head felt like it had been hit with a brick. I woke up groggy, not knowing where I was. My eyes were still closed and I was terrified to open them. I was afraid of what I might see. I was nauseous, and it felt like the room was on an axle spinning frantically. I couldn't hear anything except my own breathing and I struggled to get my brain to function ... it was proving difficult with the nausea and pain in my head. Wherever I was, it was quiet, but the stench is probably what was making me sick. It smelled like a combination of rotten food and urine. I tried to move my hands and realized I couldn't. I had to open my eyes. Once I focused in the darkness, I realized that I was lying on a bed, my hands taped together and cuffed to the headboard. Panic settled in and I tried to scream. But when my scream came out muffled, I quickly realized that I was gagged. Suddenly I remembered what had happened: somebody grabbed me. But who?

Suddenly, I heard voices coming from the other side of the door. Then I heard the lock turning, and the door slowly opened. The light coming from the doorway silhouetted the figure coming in the room, and I was blinded by the brightness spilling into the room. The dark figure was walking toward me. I still couldn't make out who it was, but there was something familiar about this person. I knew it was male ... and then suddenly, I knew who it was. Once that realization hit me, panic and terror don't even come close to describing what I felt.

"It's about time you woke up," he said. "I was worried. I thought that dose of Rohypnol that Skid gave you was too much and we were gonna lose you. Lucky for him that didn't happen. However, so very unlucky for you."

I recognized that voice. It was Mark. I was still dazed and a little uncertain. Why would he be doing this to me?

The next thing I knew, something metal and cold was sliding up between my lips and the gag that was covering my mouth. The knife cut the gag with little effort and I was able to speak.

CHAPTER 31

Caden

I pulled up to the house and found Reb's car gone. Where were they? He knew I was coming. I went inside and there were grocery bags all over the counter, but nothing was put away; everything was still in the bags. Something was wrong. I called Emma, and I could hear the phone ringing. Her purse was on the kitchen counter, with her phone sticking out of the top. Fuck. I called Rebel – no answer. I sent him a text.

> What the fuck is going on?

No response. Now I was frantic. I called Hawk, and he answered on the first ring.

"Hey man, have you heard from Rebel?" I asked.

"No, why?"

"Fuck man, I don't know. They are not here! There are groceries on the counter still in the bags. Emma's purse is here with her phone. I can't get ahold of anyone."

"What do you need me to do?" he asked.

"I don't know. Stay by your phone. Try to get Reb on the phone. See what you can find out. Call Skeeter and Peyton. See if they know anything. Get back to me as soon as you can."

"Will do." He hung up. For the first time in my life, I was at a loss. I didn't know what to do or what to think. Even when my parents died, I'd had a plan. I always had a plan.

Fifteen minutes after I arrived at the house, the door flew open and Rebel came in.

"What the fuck man, where's Emma?" I yelled. I didn't have the patience for hellos, I had to know where my girl was.

"Ice, man, I did everything I could. She was only out of my sight for a minute." He was a mess, and I could tell he was as distraught as I was.

"What? What? Tell me now!" I was losing what little patience I had.

"Someone took her. She's gone, and I have been driving everywhere trying to find her. It's as if she has vanished."

"I told you not to leave her! What in the hell were you two doing up here?! You had one job: keep Emma safe!"

"I know, I know ... she was safe. She wanted to go grocery shopping today; we were running low on food. She bumped into a guy in the store that had a devil tattoo on his neck. We were both in the produce section getting things we needed. I went over to her to make sure she was ok – she was rattled, but fine. When we left, there was a Harley in the parking lot, but it never left and so I was sure we weren't followed. We got back to the house and started carrying in groceries. I was coming in as she was going out. We were separated for mere seconds. Then I heard her scream and saw a black SUV pulling out of the drive. It was the same SUV that followed us that day from her apartment, I am sure of it. I tried to follow them, but lost them. I'm sorry, Ice ... more sorry than you will ever know."

I could feel the blood in my face disappear. I was trying to process what I've been told. Emma was gone. Grayson had her, and I had no fucking clue where she could be.

I was so pissed at Rebel, I couldn't even look at him. I stepped outside and called Hawk. He answered, "Nothing yet, Ice."

"Grayson has her."

"What? Where in the hell was Rebel?"

"He was here. I don't get it, Hawk. Why would he let this happen?"

"Ice, I know you are upset, but I know what you are implying and I don't believe it. Rebel would never rat us out to another club. We are his family, his life. You know his past history. No, I don't believe it."

"Then how could this happen? How did he just let them take her away? If he didn't rat us out, then who did?"

"I don't know if that's what happened. Get yourself back here and we will figure this thing out. "

Defeated, I replied, "They got us, Hawk. They outsmarted us. All the planning that we have done ... they just bought into it to fool us. They beat us at our own game. We need to find her. We need to find her now!"

"We'll find her, I promise you that. I'll get some guys together and stake out the Satans' clubhouse, Grayson's house, and his workplace. We're on it."

"Thanks man. I doubt that he is keeping her anywhere nearby. He will take her where he feels comfortable, which means they are probably on their way back to Edinboro. Keep your eyes and ears open. We are on lockdown. Bring everyone in, Skeeter and Peyton too. Send someone to Slippery Rock to bring Ari home. I'll be back in town in four hours."

"Ok, Ice. If you need anything else, all you gotta do is call." Hawk hung up and I turned toward Rebel. He was beside himself, but it left me no comfort.

"What the hell is going on here, Reb?" I knew Hawk didn't believe my suspicions, but I had to know for sure. "Is there something you need to tell me?"

"Ice, no, it's not what you are thinking. I swear!" he pleaded.

I still was not buying it, so I probed some more. "Then why don't you explain to me how they found her in a place that I was sure they didn't know even existed? Someone had to rat, Reb ... was it you?"

"Hell no! I would never rat out our club, no matter who was involved. Ice, I've been your sergeant at arms for three years now;

you know me better than anyone. Do you really believe I would turn on you?"

"For a price, even the most loyal brother would rat."

"I'm no rat!" he yelled. "You asked me to watch your girl and I did! I did everything I could. We were fucking carrying in groceries, the last thing I expected was for someone to take her!" He paused briefly and added, "Look man, I know you are upset. If it were me, I would be going batshit crazy right now. But we are wasting time arguing about this. Let's get back to Edinboro and find your girl!"

He was right on so many levels. I wanted, no, I *needed* to blame someone. But really, I had nobody to blame but myself. I should have been here with her. I took a deep breath and said, "Reb man, I'm sorry. I'm just so fucking lost. If I lose her now, because of this, I don't know what I will fucking do."

"I know. Come on, we need to head back to Edinboro. You go ahead and I'll get Emma's things together and be right behind you." He hesitated for a minute and then said, "Ice, I know I let you down. I'm sorry."

I walked over to him and patted him on the back. "You did the best you could. I don't blame you for this. I blame myself. I thought we had them. I underestimated Grayson. This is my fault."

I got on my bike and was back on the road to Edinboro.

CHAPTER 32

Emma

"Mark? Why are you doing this?" I asked in the darkness. "Where am I? Why am I bound?" Silence. I couldn't take it anymore. "Say something, damnit!" I yelled.

Instead of responding, he laughed. He was scaring me. Nothing about this was funny, and his laughter was terrifying. It wasn't the normal reserved laugh that I was used to. No, this laugh sounded as if it came from Satan himself. Terrified at what he would do next, I cringed as he leaned down to me and brushed his nose against my ear. Chills ran down my body. I didn't know what to do, so I just stayed silent and still. He then whispered in my ear, "You don't get to ask questions, bitch. I'm done playing it your way. From now on, my dear Emma, you are going do things my way." He took his hand and ran it down my body, lingering and touching my breasts, down my stomach, straight to the waistband of my jeans. He fumbled with the button and zipper until they finally came free.

"He's going to rape me," I thought to myself. *"Oh God no, please no. If he does this, I know I won't survive it."*

"Mark, please. Please don't do this. Let's talk this out between us. I didn't mean to hurt you. I'm so sorry," I pleaded. He removed his hand from my jeans and suddenly his fist made a beeline for my face. Ouch, that hurt like hell! My head was spinning and the darkness started to consume me. My face was screaming with pain. No, no, no! I refused to let him win. I was slowly fading, but I knew that I had to stay awake. I couldn't lose my head now. So, I fought with everything in me to remain conscious.

The room was extremely dark, and I couldn't see him clearly. But he smelled. His smell, combined with the stench of the room, was making me sick. I could barely make him out, but he was so close to me that I sensed that he was not dressed in his usual suit and tie. He was always so polished, but the man before me was more like a savage. He put his head in my face and smirked at me – it was the scariest expression I had ever seen on him.

"I told you, you don't speak. If you do, I'll hit you again." He paused for a moment and then continued. "You know how long I have been waiting for this? To get you here, like this?" He gestured toward me lying on the bed. "It was all I thought about when I was working Brianne over. That little bitch, she was gonna open her fat mouth and tell you everything about me. I had to teach that little cunt a lesson. Then you had to go and hook up with the Knights. So, my darling fiancée, now it's your turn. I'm gonna break you. Use you over and over again and then send you back to those assholes."

Oh God, Brianne. Is she still alive? I wanted to speak, but the pain in my face was a reminder to keep my mouth shut. Mark seemed like he was in the mood to talk, so hopefully if I didn't make him mad, I would find out why he was doing this.

Roughly, he push his hand down my jeans, his fingers jabbing into me. He was pushing violently, making my core burn and throb with pain. *Please stop. Caden, where are you? Please find me.*

"Why are you so fucking dry, bitch? You were always that way when we were together. Wasn't I enough for you? Didn't I turn you on like your badass biker Iceman does? You think I don't know about the two of you? I've known about the two of you a lot longer than I have known you, sweetheart. You better get those pussy juices flowing baby, or you are in for a long and painful night."

I couldn't move. I couldn't speak. I hurt everywhere, and I was terrified. I just kept praying that he wouldn't rape me. As if God listened, Mark suddenly stopped pushing against my core and looked back up at me. He got this evil look in his eyes and said,

"But first, I want you to know what kind of man you've been shacking up with."

He got up from the bed and walked over to the other side of the room, disappearing into the darkness. I heard the sound of a button being pushed and then the room is illuminated with the light from a TV. At first the screen is fuzzy, but then suddenly I was watching Caden at the Knights' clubhouse, hanging all over some blonde. They were kissing. Mark said, "This video was taken last night. Apparently the Knights had a big party. Funny you weren't there. Why is that?"

Devastated, I looked away from the TV screen. I just couldn't watch any more. Mark grabbed my head and turned it toward the TV again and held me there, making me watch every second of Caden with this other woman. My heart broke into a million pieces and I realized that he wasn't coming for me. Nobody was. I was utterly alone at the hands of a madman. *I love you, Caden!*

"So, now that you know that your big bad biker is a cheating asshole, perhaps you will give me your undivided attention." He smiled and mused, "Where to begin? I had so many plans for this moment and I have to say, I am a little overwhelmed." He left the video on and walked over to the bed and sat down next to me. Then he added, "I need to touch you." He ran his hands down my body and I tried so hard not to flinch, but I couldn't help it – his touch repulsed me. His reaction surprised me. Instead of getting angry at my reaction to his touch, he gave me a wicked smile and continued. Oh my God, he was enjoying my disgust for him. What a sick bastard!

"Well, my little bitch, I think this is the first time since we have been together that you have actually gotten me this hard. I'm ready to fuck you now." My stomach turned and I felt as if I was going to throw up. He roughly pulled my jeans off me along with my panties. He pulled out his knife again and slid it up the center of my shirt and bra, slicing them in two. I was completely naked, and I had never felt more vulnerable. Tears started to roll down my cheek and I started to cry uncontrollably. He slapped me, hard. "Keep crying, baby. Cry out for me, 'cause I know you are gonna enjoy this as much as I will." I started shaking my head no, which only angered him more, and he slapped me again. Still, the pain radiating through my head wasn't nearly as bad as the pain I was feeling in my heart. Caden had abandoned me.

I felt that I had nothing left. Even if I got out of this alive, I would have nothing left. I wished that Mark would just get this over with. I had given up. I went completely still, and my crying stopped. I had no more fight in me.

Mark could sense my defeat and suddenly he backed off of me. "What the fuck, Emma, you are ruining this for me." He began to pace and then turned back toward me. "Fight back, you little bitch. This reminds me of when we were together before. You always just laid there. You were a lousy lay. I want the excitement. I want you to claw at me to stop. I want to hear you cry, damnit!" I was silent and he just stared at me, infuriated. He raised his hand and struck me again, and again. I did the one thing he didn't want me to do: I just laid there, not making a sound, not even crying. Suddenly, he turned away from me and angrily stormed out of the room.

So now I was naked and alone again. The room was freezing, and I couldn't do anything to cover myself. I was hungry and thirsty. I glanced over at the TV and realized that Mark had left the video playing. The images of Caden and that blonde chick kissing were playing over and over again. I tried not to think about my current situation and instead stared at the screen. I couldn't take my eyes off them, and my heartbreak was getting worse and worse with each kiss. Suddenly something caught my eye, and I looked a little more closely at the girl. She was wearing my clothes. And my boots! I know they're mine because I left them at the clubhouse. Wait a minute ... he was acting! Caden was always very casual and easygoing with me, but he was forcing this. I could see it now, on his face. Even she seems a bit uncomfortable. This was a show. This was staged for Mark's benefit. I just know it. They must have wanted to make Mark think that I was at the clubhouse. Suddenly, I had hope. I still doubted I was ever going to leave this place alive, but I knew one thing for sure. I was not going to go down without a fight. Bring it on, Mark Grayson – you will never be half the man that Caden Jackson is.

CHAPTER 33

Caden

Fuck, fuck, fuck! I can't take this waiting game. I'd been back at the clubhouse for an hour now. My boys were busy scoping out the Satans' compound, but I'd heard nothing. I was losing all sense of sanity. It had been five fuckin' hours, and nothing. Grayson was good, I'd give him that. He had left no trail, no sign of either of them. For the first time in my life, I didn't know where to turn. I had nobody to call and nobody to question. How in the hell was I supposed to get answers?

I needed to keep it together. I couldn't lose my head over this. We *would* find her. I just had to keep telling myself that so I could continue to think clearly. I needed to stop beating myself up about this, as well. But how could I? I failed her.

I'd been trying to get ahold of Skeeter for a couple of hours now, but his phone just goes to voicemail. As I grabbed my cell phone and look down, trying to find Skeeter's number again, it rang in my hand: the caller ID read REBEL. Thank fuck! "What do you got?" I tried to keep calm because he could be giving me bad news or good news. I had to keep my composure no matter what he says.

The voice on the phone wasn't Rebel, and it sent chills down my spine. "I got your girl, Iceman," he hissed with distaste.

What the fuck? How did he get Rebel's phone? "You fucking cocksucker! You better not have harmed a single hair on her head, you son of a bitch!"

"Take it easy there, Ice. You piss me off and I'll do more to her than I have already done." His voice sounds like a snake slithering across the asphalt; he was putting me on edge. This man was Satan reincarnate.

I needed to proceed with caution. I took a minute to compose myself and then calmly, I asked, "What do you want? And while you are at it, why don't you fucking tell me how you found her."

He laughed. "Now you are asking the right questions." He paused and then continued proudly, "Well Cade, perhaps it is time that you understand why I am making your life a living hell. You have thought all this time that this is about Emma. You are so fucking wrong. I've had my eyes on you for a very long time. I know all your club safe houses and probably more about your club than you do." He paused and asked, "Have you figured it out yet?"

"Figured what out?" I asked, confused.

"This has been about you since the beginning."

Me? What in the hell?

"I can hear the wheels turning in your brain right now. You are wondering why in the hell this is all about you, aren't you?" He waited for me to answer.

Calmly I said, "Yes."

He laughed again and it echoed through the phone like Satan himself. It was unnerving, but I kept telling myself that if I wanted Emma safe, I had to keep calm. He said, "So, let me ask you something. Do you remember Ace?"

Ace? What did he have to do with all this? Ace died ten years ago. "Of course I do. What does he have to do with this?" I asked.

"Again, you are asking the right questions. If I understand your history with Ace, he was your sponsor into the club. He was your mentor, and after your parents were killed, he was like a surrogate father to you. Am I right?"

"Yes, that's right."

"Well, he was a fucking asshole to me. I am his son, his own flesh and blood, and he gave me up. He said he didn't want this life for me. Instead of being a good father and taking his own son under his wing, he took you. He chose my brother over me."

Brother? What the fuck?

"I bet you are really confused now."

"You are not my brother," I said confidently.

He laughed again. I wished he would just get to the point. None of this was making any sense. "Actually, you are wrong. I am your brother. You and I share the same father. Ace was your father." What in the hell was fucking going on?

"That's impossible."

"It's not. I am two years older than you. Your mom was pregnant before she married your dad. She and Ace were in love, and it was always my guess that she would have married him if her parents hadn't interfered."

"If what you are saying is true, why is it such a big deal that you have a younger brother? What the hell did I ever do to you?"

"You fucking stole my life! My mother was a junkie whore who couldn't take care of a fish, let alone a kid. She pawned me off on Ace. I was 14 when Ace was voted in as VP. He was convinced that the biker life was not an ideal situation for a young teenager, so he pawned me off with his sister who lived in New York. You may look at it as him doing me a favor - that he cared. But I know different. He didn't want me anymore, plain and simple. Then, years later, he takes you in. You got the life I wanted. Now, I am taking your life away. It's that simple."

"But why Emma, or Brianne for that matter? They are innocent in all this!"

"Brianne found out about my connection to you. She was going to tell Emma, and I couldn't let that happen. She has been dealt with. Emma, on the other hand, is a different story. At first, my connection to Emma was purely to get her to marry me. You see, I've always known about the two of you. But then, when she broke our engagement and chose you over me, it was a whole new ball game. She has to pay as well."

"So what do you want?" I was literally sick to my stomach. I knew nothing of having a brother. My parents had never said anything about it, nor had Ace. I felt like the walls were closing in around me and I was suffocating.

"This is what's going to happen. You have twenty-four hours to make your choice. Listen real fucking good, you worthless piece of shit. If you want Emma to live, you die. Very simple. It's your life for hers. Now I can't promise that no harm will come to her, but I promise she will live. I'll see to it. If you don't give me the life I am due, then she disappears – and don't think I've forgotten about your dear sister, Ari. She's a fucking beauty and it makes my cock twitch just thinking about sinking into her. Should I continue, or have you got my fucking point?"

"I hear you loud and fuckin' clear." I had heard every word he had said. All of this was just insane. But, I had no choice. I would not let Emma or Ari suffer another minute because of me. Hopefully someday they would understand.

"Twenty-four hours, brother. You can call me on Reb's phone. It was nice of him to leave it in the car when I took Emma. Remind me to thank him." He laughed again and then added, "Oh, before I forget. You have five minutes to clear out your clubhouse. Or everyone inside will go up in smoke with it." Right before he hung up the phone I could hear him laughing again.

I ran outside my office and started yelling. "Get everyone out! Now! It's a bomb!" I checked every possible room in the clubhouse I could think of. Honey and a couple of the boys were at the bar. They frantically ran out the front door. I called over to Honey and said, "Anyone upstairs?"

"No," she called back. "Ice, everyone is out. Let's go!"

I followed her out the door. A few seconds after we reached the parking lot, the building blew.

Looking at the devastation before me, I knew I only had one choice. I pulled my phone out of my pocket and dialed. He answered on the first ring, which was no surprise to me. His satanic laugh echoed in my ear. I spoke distinctly into the phone, "Message received. You got me."

TO BE CONTINUED…

ICE PLAYLIST

Born to Be Wild, Steppenwolf
I'm Eighteen, Alice Cooper
Whole Lotta Love, Led Zeplin
Smokin' In The Boys Room, Motley Crue
Riders On the Storm, The Doors
Make It Rain, Ed Sheeran
Love is My Religion, Franky Perez & The Forest Rangers
Turn the Page, Bob Seager
Wanted Dead Or Alive, Bon Jovi
Pour Some Sugar On Me, Def Leppard
Sympathy for The Devil, Rolling Stones
Whiskey Man, Molly Hatchett
Freebird, Lynard Skynyrd
Bad to The Bone, George Thorogood & The Destroyers
You Shook Me All Night Long, AC/DC
Ghosts of Days Gone By, Alter Bridge
Lick it up, KISS
Come Together, Aerosmith
Come Healing, Leonard Cohen
The Sound of Silence, Disturbed

ACKNOWLEDGEMENTS

First of all, I would like to thank my friends and family. Without their support, I never would've had the courage and the vision to bring to life Caden and Emma's story.

I would like to thank Red Horn, may you rest in peace. It was an honor knowing you. You gave me a true glimpse inside the MC world and really helped me establish the heart of this story.

I would like to thank the residents of the towns of Waterford and Edinboro, Pennsylvania. Your hospitality while I was visiting and doing my research went above and beyond what I ever expected.

Also, I'd like to thank Hannah Hall. Your comments and suggestions during all the writing stages of this book truly helped shape the outcome. It makes my writing so much easier to have someone to share my thoughts and ideas.

I would also like to thank Alicia Freeman. Your PR abilities are amazing and I couldn't ask for a better personal assistant. You have opened up so many doors for me. You are a pleasure to work with and I could not be more grateful.

And finally, I would like to thank Ellie and Carl Augsburger for their insightful ideas, creative cover designs, marketing materials and comprehensive editing. I am blessed to have such a talented creative design and editing team. You guys rock!

ABOUT THE AUTHOR

Amy Cecil writes contemporary and historical romance. Her novel, *ICE* is the first in the *Knights of Silence MC* series. When she isn't writing, she is spending time with her husband, friends and various pets.

She is a member of the Romance Writers of America (RWA) and the Published Authors Network (PAN). She was a winner in the 2015 NanNoWriMo writing contest and a nominee in Metamorph Publishing's Indie Book 2016 contest in historical romance.

She lives in North Carolina with her husband, Kevin, and their three dogs, Hobbes, Koda and Karma and her horse, Baylee.

This is Amy's third novel.

KNIGHTS OF SILENCE SERIES

Amy is currently working on Book II of the Knights of Silence MC Series, *Ice on Fire*. In the meantime, she wants to hear from you!

Amazon: www.amazon.com/author/amycecil
Goodreads: goodreads.com/author/show/5888015.Amy_Cecil
Webpage: acecil65.wix.com/amycecil
Facebook: facebook.com/novelideasbyamy
Playlist:www.youtube.com/playlist?list=PLUovHfuDYnHhZViCtd ot1Q2nX9Prihoy7
Trailer: youtu.be/hkuMqv3oFzk

DON'T FORGET…

If you've read *ICE* and loved it, then please leave a review. Authors love reading reviews!

Made in United States
North Haven, CT
05 July 2023

38586260R00120